FRANNIE in PIECES

DELIA EPHRON

FRANNIE iN PIECES

DRAWINGS BY CHAD W. BECKERMAN

LAURA GERINGER BOOKS

HARPER TEEN

An Imprint of HarperCollinsPublishers

HarperTeen is an imprint of HarperCollins Publishers.

Frannie in Pieces

Text copyright © 2007 by South of Pico Productions Inc.

Illustrations copyright © 2007 by Chad W. Beckerman

www.harperteen.com

Library of Congress Cataloging-in-Publication Data

Ephron, Delia.

Frannie in pieces / Delia Ephron ; drawings by Chad W. Beckerman. — 1st ed.

p. cm.

Summary: When fifteen-year-old Frannie's father dies, only a mysterious jigsaw
puzzle that he leaves behind can help her come to terms with his death.

ISBN-10: 0-06-074716-1 (trade bdg.) — ISBN-13: 978-0-06-074716-9 (trade bdg.)
ISBN-10: 0-06-074717-X (lib. bdg.) — ISBN-13: 978-0-06-074717-6 (lib. bdg.)

[1. Fathers and daughters—Fiction. 2. Death—Fiction. 3. Grief—Fiction.
4. Jigsaw puzzles—Fiction. 5. Space and time—Fiction.] I. Beckerman, Chad, ill.
II. Title.

PZ7.E7246Fr 2007   2007010909
[Fic]—dc22   CIP
                                                                         AC

Typography by Chad W. Beckerman

1 2 3 4 5 6 7 8 9 10

First Edition

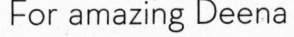
For amazing Deena

FRANNIE in PIECES

1

Do you know what it says on a tube of toothpaste? In small print? You have to read the small print because they never tell you anything scary in large print. Large print is what they want you to see. Here's what the large print says: FOR BEST RESULTS, SQUEEZE TUBE FROM THE BOTTOM AND FLATTEN AS YOU GO UP. But the important stuff is small. Tiny. *If more than used for brushing is accidentally swallowed, get medical help or contact a Poison Control Center right away.*

You can die from toothpaste.

I tell my mom this at dinner. Although I'm not eating. I tell her I have a stomachache. Which might be true. My mom says that I don't have to eat, but I do have to sit with them. While stuck there, I focus on things that have no meaning to me, like my stepfather's hair. Jenna and I have discussed Mel's hair and the possibility of putting a hidden camera in the bathroom to record exactly how he gets it to do what it does. I suspect that he wets it and combs it forward so it hangs like strings over his eyes. It's hay colored and not too thick, by the way. Then he parts it on the right, and, with a flip of the comb, swirls it left so it dips over his forehead and swoops up again. Strangely, it retains its comb marks. Jenna thinks gel is involved.

Have you ever noticed, in the movies, when the point is that no one in a family is speaking—not because they're mad at each other, but because, between the kids and the parents, there is zero communication—the family is often silent at the dinner table, with only the sound of forks scraping plates? Well, life at my house is not like that. We have nothing in common but my mom won't shut up. Probably because she's laying on a veneer. Veneer, if you look it up in the dictionary, means "a thin surface layer. A façade." Listen to her: "There were fresh anemones today, I suppose they forced them or flew them in from a Central American country because they're at least three weeks early and they cost a complete fortune, I couldn't possibly make a profit on them, but those flowers are beautiful, it's like they have black eyes with long curly lashes, some of the petals are persimmon or colors you'd see only on a fish, and how about that delicate fringy leaf, like each flower is wearing a ruffled collar."

"Toothpaste can kill you," I say.

Now there is silence. I have achieved silence. You see, my mom can talk a streak, but eventually she has to take a breath, and when she does, I'm there.

"What makes you think that?" she asks eventually.

"It says so on the package."

"I bet you'd have to swallow a whole tube," says Mel.

"I'm sure he's right," she chimes in.

"In the Middle Ages they didn't have toothpaste." Mel teaches medieval history. "Queen Elizabeth the First brushed her teeth with pomegranate juice. That's why she never smiled for any of her portraits. She had hardly any teeth left."

"How fascinating," says my mom.

"It doesn't say you'd have to swallow a whole tube. It says, 'If more than used for brushing . . .' That's about two inches."

"I hope you're not going to stop brushing, too."

The "too" refers to my having given up silverware and china. My place setting is now entirely disposable. More on that later.

My father died. He died on March 24th. Two months ago. A week before my birthday. He lived in a house eight blocks away. I always visited him after school on Wednesdays.

"Hey, Dad, it's me."

There was no answer. My dad never forgets that Wednesdays belong to us, but occasionally something comes up and he knows that I know he'll be back. I dumped my parka and my backpack on the couch on top of the magazines. My dad reads—I mean, read—*Newsweek* and *Time*, plus a magazine called *Fine Woodworking* and *Condé Nast Traveler*, and he always left them lying around. "He lives like a college student," I heard my mom tell her friend Rachel on the telephone. I don't know what Mom meant exactly, but it's not true. Wasn't true. He loves junk. Loved. Great junk. Things other people didn't want. Things sitting on the curb waiting for Thursday.

In Hudson Glen, New York, where we live, Thursday is pick-up-big-garbage day. Which means that on Wednesday evenings my dad and I would go foraging. "We see the beauty, don't we, Frannie?" His couch is bamboo. Someone threw out a perfectly good bamboo couch except for a few gouges in the arms. And his coffee table is an old blue metal trunk with rusted locks. In the corner of the living room stands a stringless guitar, slightly warped. "Look at the shape, Frannie. Look what weather can do." There is a ton of other stuff—a doll's arm, a few large dominoes, a broken radio in green plastic, a cracked clock with the works showing, an old-fashioned black telephone with a circular dial and finger holes. My dad said, "Take away use and you have art." That's a very cool observation, and you should think about it for at least a minute. All the small objects we found dump digging, which is just what it sounds like, tramping through the dump searching for treasure. Everything we collected we appreciate, and I'm sorry to say my mom does not. "One putteth down what one doth not understand." That's not in the Bible, but it should be.

That afternoon the milk carton was sitting on the kitchen counter. Opened. My dad is always forgetting to put things back. I'm like him that way.

So I put the milk back in the refrigerator, trying not to look too closely at what was inside. My dad never covers anything. It's like he never heard of Saran wrap, Baggies, or plastic containers. If he eats spaghetti, he pours what's left into a bowl and pops it, topless, into the fridge. Things grow fuzz and turn strange colors.

Fudgsicles are the only things in my dad's freezer, and he stocks them for me. There's no room for anything else because, unlike my mom's, his freezer does not automatically defrost. It looks like the ice age. After taking a Fudgsicle (I had to chip away some ice to get the freezer to close again), I cleared space on the couch, sat down, and considered my options. Homework. English class. Read thirty pages of *Lord of the Flies*. U.S. history, thirty-five pages, and answer some questions about the Civil War. While doing either assignment, I could apply my favorite technique, reading for five minutes, daydreaming for five minutes. Or I could watch the light. "Watch the light, Frannie." Imagine having a dad who tells you to sit around and watch light. That is another reason why he is a totally rare father. Was. Was, was, was.

My dad's windows face south. At three thirty P.M. on this clear windy day, dots of bright white were scattered like confetti across the floor, thanks to the warm afternoon light filtering through the trees outside Dad's window. "Light is rarely boring and never still, right, Frannie?" A beam of sun obliterated a corner of the coffee table, chopping it right off. I focused on the middle distance, on bits of feathery dust floating in air.

Spacing out on the light, I finished the Fudgsicle and dug into the nuts and raisins that my dad keeps in a kitchen canister. I alternate: First one cashew, then an almond and raisin simultaneously. While so pleasantly engaged . . . Don't you like to speak grandly now and then? It makes your life sound impressive. Compare "while so pleasantly engaged" with "while pigging out," another way to describe my activities.

While so pleasantly engaged, I called Jenna.

Jenna and I met in the playground in Reservoir Park when Jordan Keener beaned her with a shovel and I pushed him down. Jenna and I don't remember this, but our moms do. We were three years old, and we've been in school together ever since kindergarten, although not always in the same class. In fifth grade the teachers decided we were too cliquey, so in sixth grade they split us up. Now that we're in ninth grade, we don't have any of the same classes, but we meet before school, at lunch, and after.

We're not anything alike. Our looks, for starters. I have dark-brown, frizzy hair. No product can tame it. Believe me, I've tried everything on the market, and once Jenna ironed it. No kidding, I leaned my head on the board and she ironed my hair, using the setting for polyester. After a minute she had to stop because 1) we were laughing too hard, and 2) my hair started to sizzle. Jenna's nickname for me is Wildwoman. You've seen television commercials in which a glamorous model or actress swings her hair back and forth. "I use Lustro-Sheen," swish, the hair falls forward over one eye. She pushes a hand through it or flips her head down and up, boom, it swings over to the other side. Or she walks away twitching her butt, and her hair obligingly dances about in a sexy, gentle way. Well, my hair won't swish or flip or dance. It's a shoulder-length hedge. You wouldn't stick your hand in a hedge, would you? Enough said.

Don't you have a body part that is your burden to bear? Once you start thinking about it, you can't stop. I really hate my hair. I guess that's why I notice everyone else's hair, including Mel's.

If you have straight hair, I will envy you until I die. Jenna has straight hair. I try not to be green with jealousy.

Did you ever play "What's your favorite body part?" It's not a game exactly. It was a way, in sixth grade, that some kids tried to make other kids feel bad. (Sixth grade was the meanest year so far by far.) The kids who were developed knew I had nothing to brag about and they did. "I love my breasts," Sukie Jameson would say, just as I was thinking that perhaps my ankles were my favorite body part and was even considering crying about it. That was before I had something to cry about. Maybe God said, "I'll give you something to cry about," and that's why my dad died. Because once I was so idiotic that I almost cried about my best body part being my ankles. They're very trim. My legs aren't too bad either. Shapely. La, la, la. I look good in short shorts, it's true. What I don't like is that my hips are wide, and, right above my waist, one rib pokes out more than the others. I finally got breasts, but I think they are too far apart. Jenna's are round and perky, although we both have small ones and that's a bond.

Jenna takes ballet. She can dance on point. Her posture is excellent, her neck long and swanlike. She has tiny features, skin white as snow; and her cheeks get a natural pink glow when she's excited—

how much luck is that? She has black eyes that slant slightly up and thick black brows. I am not so delicate, facewise. My face is long. My dad once showed me a famous portrait by Modigliani, and I've been worried ever since that I look mournful like the woman in that painting. My nose has a slight bump in it, and my eyes are brown, which fills me with a certain amount of despair. Brown is the most boring color (how often did you take that color out of the Crayola box?), especially boring if your hair is brown, too. My mother says I have huge saucer eyes, full of feeling (what does that mean?). My dad loves my dimples, one in each cheek. Loved my dimples. When you've got dimples, cute is the most you can aspire to. Fact, not opinion.

Jenna can do a backbend. And splits. And hold her leg up so it touches her forehead, while I cannot touch my toes.

What I like to do is draw. My dad kept an old tomato can with sharpened pencils on the coffee table trunk. Things may have rotted in his refrigerator, but the pencils were always sharp. "They're for you, Frannie, in case inspiration strikes." I don't like to draw nature—objects of beauty like a tree, bird, or flower. I like to draw banal things. Banal, if you look it up in the dictionary, means "completely ordinary."

I might have drawn the milk carton on my dad's counter.

Mel once looked at my drawing of a wastebasket with crumpled paper inside and said, "Why did you draw that?" When I ignored him, my mom prodded, "Mel asked you a question, Frannie." I didn't want to tell him because I don't want him to know anything about me, so I said, "I don't know." But afterward I thought about his question. I draw banal things because they suggest a story. Maybe there's a love letter in that wastebasket, or that wastebasket is full because the housekeeper forgot to empty it because she's downstairs locking lips with the gardener. Rosanna, who comes to clean once a week, doesn't even know Cliff (whom Mom calls our "lawn man"), because Rosanna cleans on Monday and he mows on Thursday. But maybe they have met and I don't know it. Maybe he forgot his rake and returned on Monday to get it. See what I mean?

Did I get sidetracked? I guess, because I'm telling you about the day my father died. After I watched the light, I phoned Jenna on her cell. My mom forces me to carry one so she can find me at all times. My dad doesn't like them. He says—

STOP! No more of that. My dad *didn't* like cell phones. He doesn't say, he *said*. Past tense. My brain is not behaving. But is it my brain that won't behave or my heart? It's hard to keep the body parts straight. I mean, speaking of a person who bit the dust, a doctor might announce, "His heart stopped." But sometimes the doctor says, "He's brain-dead." I say, "Which is it? Make up your mind. Which does you in, brain or heart?"

I have to think about that.

Sarah's mom, Katrine, had breast cancer. She had horrible chemotherapy where her hair fell out and her eyes were rimmed in red, as if someone had outlined them with a sharp red pencil, the type used for grading papers. I would always say to Jenna, "That would be so sad if Katrine died." If any grown-up died, it was supposed to be Katrine.

When I phoned Jenna she answered, "Hi, Frannie."

"Where are you?"

"Where do you think?"

LIPS is the answer to that question. Jenna's nickname is Liplady. Liplady and Wildwoman. That's us.

LIPS, a store in the Hudson Glen mall, sells makeup, and the sign brags, "Over two thousand colors of lipstick." It's possible Jenna has tried every one. She's been fixated on makeup since forever. When we were little, we would investigate her mom's makeup drawer. Her mom's a minor slob (fact, not opinion), kind of like my dad, and kept her makeup jars and tubes jumbled up, lots of them without tops. Our hands went into the drawer clean and came out smeared with rouge or shadow or mascara or gloss. Jenna would "design our faces," that's what she called it. I might end up with green eye shadow, dusty rose cheeks, and lips outlined in plum with pink inside. Jenna usually painted her own face on a red theme. Afterward we'd stand in front of a tall mirror, arms linked. Jenna would say, "Cheese," and we'd smile as if someone was taking our photo.

"What's going on, your dad's not there?" asked Jenna on the phone.

"Right."

"OhmyGod, Waldo's outside. I'm going to follow him." She hung up.

Gone. She was gone.

I was forced into homework, but my feet hurt. I was wearing my cowboy boots, and the nail on my pinky toe was cutting into the toe next to it, so I decided to air out my feet. I pulled off my boots and socks and examined my toes. On my left foot, my toes naturally overlap—is this interesting? Probably not, but it has to do with the story—and when my pinky toenail is the slightest bit long, it stabs the toe next to it and frequently draws blood. It's amazing the kind of pain a pinky toenail can cause, so I decided to go into my dad's bathroom to get his nail clippers. I wasn't sure I would find them. His medicine cabinet was only slightly less disgusting than his refrigerator. As I walked toward the bathroom, I heard a screen door bang, so I yelled,

"Hi, Dad," one second before I saw him. He was on the bathroom floor, not sitting or lying, more in a heap, and his eyes were wide open, startled. Maybe God personally came to get him, and my dad was shocked to see him. I'm getting rattled trying to tell this story (although I shouldn't call it a story because it's not a story, it's true), because what I saw then and what I figured out later or thought later or my mom told me later were different. I thought he was naked, but he wasn't, he was wearing jockey shorts. I'd seen my dad in a bathing suit but never in his underwear, and I didn't really see his underwear now. His chest was bare and his legs were bare and he was kind of folded over. I assumed he was all bare. I thought he'd been murdered. I ran outside and kept running. Eloiza Wachtel, who lives next door, heard me screaming, although I don't remember screaming. She'd just come home. It was her screen door that had banged and she was the one who called 911.

I was three blocks away when my legs gave out.

They crumpled in the middle of Bramfield Road. Five cars stopped. I was on my knees in the fast lane, no shoes, no jacket, and my foot was bleeding, not from my overlapped toes, but because I'd stepped on my dad's razor. He'd had a heart attack while he was shaving.

I was in the house two hours while my dad was dead in the bathroom and then I ran outside and left him there all alone.

2

I suppose we should talk about dead bodies.

If you've read *Little Women*, all about the sisters Meg, Jo, Beth, and Amy, you know that Beth died. If you can figure out what she died of, you've got a different book from mine. I searched and searched, but all I found were poetic phrases about fading and weakening; eventually she slipped into the valley of the shadow. That didn't satisfy me at all.

I want to gratify your curiosity. I'm sympathetic to the need, but here's all I know. One of my dad's legs was bent back and one was forward. There was fuzzy white stuff on his face. Could he have grown mold like old cheese, or had he been attacked by mold and that's why he died? Impossible, right? So why was there mold on his face? I didn't want to ask.

I haven't been in his house since that day. Once, when my mom and I drove down Rosewood Avenue on our way to the dentist, I changed the station when we passed my dad's so I'd be looking down and not out the window.

Maybe he didn't die of a heart attack. It just seemed that way.

I guess the milk was out because he'd poured some into his coffee. When he went into the bathroom in the morning to shave, he always took his coffee cup with him. I know all his habits.

According to my mom, he wanted to be cremated. She claimed that once, when they were married, they'd discussed death. Aunt Patsy, my dad's only sister, flew in from Chicago. She and my mom hadn't spoken for ten years, since the divorce. When my mom opened the door, Patsy spied me in the dining room, charged past my mom, and put her arms around me. I was holding knives and forks at the time—it's my job to set the table—and I tried not to stab her.

"He loved you so much." She said that again and again. I thought I was going to start wailing, so I concentrated on not jabbing her with the utensils. If you think about something else hard enough, you can mostly control your feelings.

After dinner she lounged on the couch and drank scotch on the rocks. She wore a poncho that she'd designed herself out of fabric she'd bought in New Delhi. She's artistic like Dad and sells her designs, although my mom said once, "She may sell them, but who buys them?" I think Mom is jealous of artists. Also Aunt Patsy drips jewelry—clunky silver chains and medallions. Whenever she waves her hand around, which she does for emphasis, they clang. She's a walking wind chime. "I'm the only one left," she moaned.

No one said anything. Then she added, "Except Frannie, of course." She dunked one very dangly bracelet into her drink by accident, and it sprinkled scotch on her poncho. "Did he have a heart condition?" asked Patsy.

"Not that I know of, but that doesn't mean anything," said my mom, giving her a paper towel soaked in club soda to prevent the scotch from staining.

"Did he?" she asked me.

"I don't know."

"Sure he did," said Mel. "You don't have a heart attack at forty-five without a heart condition. The question is—did he know he had a heart condition?"

"I wish you'd get a stress test," my mom told Mel.

"Why?" he asked.

"Just to be safe."

"What does that have to do with Dad?"

"Nothing," said Mom.

"Fine, honey, I'll get a stress test."

"Thanks, Booper." She used her pet name for him (don't ask me what it means, I have no idea) in the middle of grief. My mom may be the queen of inappropriate.

"What's a stress test?" I asked.

"They put you on a treadmill and see how your heart reacts when they increase the speed," said Aunt Patsy. "I wonder if Sean had a stress test."

"Dad would have told me."

"Not necessarily," said Mel.

"Why are we talking about this?" said my mom. "Would anyone like some decaf?"

I think something scared him. Gave him a colossal jolt. His eyes were wide open, bulging even, and don't forget the mold.

My dad was a loner. Artist slash loner. A/L. When I slept over at his place, every other weekend, we would always go out to dinner. Either for

Thai food (coconut shrimp, mee krob, and chicken on skewers with peanut sauce) or Chinese (tofu in brown sauce, sautéed stringbeans, and spare ribs). After that, we hit the movies—we took turns choosing but usually ended up at a foreign film. We were totally into foreign films, and our all-time favorite is *Il Postino*, an utterly sad Italian movie about love. Afterward I would read or watch TV and he would disappear into the shed, his studio.

He made his sculptures out of wood—blocks, triangles, circles, and abstract geometric shapes interlocked together by an ancient art called Japanese joinery in which nails and screws are not allowed. The objects were amazing, small and intricate. Sometimes the parts moved, suggesting a person, an animal, or even a machine, but usually they didn't look like anything you'd recognize in life.

After he died, lots of people came to our house for a week, mostly in the evenings. Mom's friends.

Strange. It wasn't like Mom had lost someone. Mom said they were coming for me, but I didn't want to see them. I stayed mostly in my room.

I didn't call Jenna. I heard my mom phone her mom to tell her what happened, and Jenna turned up that night. She knocked on the door. "Frannie, it's me."

I was lying on the floor trying to see if I could fit under the bed.

"What are you doing?"

"Nothing."

I squeezed underneath with just my head poking out. "What do you want?"

"I brought you *Sugarland Express*."

"Why in the world would I want to watch *Sugarland Express*?"

"I don't know," said Jenna. "I'll take it home. I brought you this, too." She handed me a large square white envelope. I had to pull myself out a little farther and prop myself up on my elbows to read the card. On the front, a tree covered with red berries appeared to float on a slick, shiny white background. Inside it, in fancy script, "My sincere condolences for your loss," and a ton of signatures, including one from my history teacher, Everett Clarkson. Tracey Millan had drawn a heart next to her name with tears dripping off it.

"Is this a valentine?"

"No."

"Then what's this heart doing there?"

"I don't know."

"That's a stupid thing to put."

"Waldo kissed me."

"What?"

"I can't believe it."

"How could you bring that up at a time like this?"

Jenna started chewing on her lower lip. She always does this when she's about to cry. Then she wrinkles her nose—I've seen it a hundred times—sniffles, and gulps. Together they sound like one gigantic hiccup. After that, waterworks. All those things happened like clockwork, one after another.

"Why are you crying? I'm the one who's supposed to be crying."

I scooted under the bed. All the way under this time. I am a turtle and this is my shell. I am a lion and this is my den. I am a fox and this is my lair. I waited until I heard my bedroom door open and close before I came out again.

3

Regarding my fifteenth birthday. It seems pathetic to bring up such an unimportant thing, but maybe you're wondering. I didn't want to celebrate it. "No cake, nothing," I told my mom as I poured some liquid Cascade into the dishwasher, closed and locked it.

"Oh, Frannie, come on, are you sure?"

I blocked her out by reading the back of the Cascade bottle. *For best results: Fill both cups completely.*

"How about just the three of us go out for a nice dinner?"

I silently read some more. *Helps keep your glasses looking like new.*

"Maybe with Jenna?" my mom added.

I moved on to the smaller print. *If swallowed or gets in mouth, rinse mouth, give a glassful of water or milk and call a Poison Control Center or doctor immediately.*

This was the first time I realized the importance of small type and how aware of it you should be. "Mom, can you die from Cascade?"

My mom took the plastic bottle and read for herself. "Interesting," she remarked.

Interesting? How about alarming?

Maybe Dad's dishwasher hadn't rinsed off the Cascade. Suppose his mug was actually coated with Cascade residue and, when he drank his coffee, he got poisoned? Maybe he knew he was having a detergent reaction, read the bottle, and took the milk out to counteract it. But he died anyway and that's why the milk carton was still sitting there. Although I guess not, because Dad didn't use his dishwasher. He kept his camera in it, don't ask me why, and his binoculars, and several paperback books including one of his favorites: *The Sibley Guide to Birds*.

Consider this carefully. A liquid soap invented for the purpose of cleaning glasses, mugs, bowls, knives, forks, and spoons is potentially poisonous. I mean, what were they thinking? "I don't want my dishes washed in the dishwasher," I told Mom.

"Oh, Frannie, I don't think there's any danger."

Like she'd know. Had she been expecting Dad to drop dead? No, probably she was expecting Sarah's mom, Katrine, to die, like all the rest of us, but Katrine is fine. Her hair is growing back, and last month Katrine and Sarah went snowboarding.

From that day forth I've been using paper plates and cups, and plastic utensils. I bought them myself.

I thought I had thrown my mom off the birthday trail, but when I was in the bathroom investigating a new pimple, she knocked on the door. "Do you think your dad would want you to skip your birthday?"

It's an extreme presumption to suggest what a dead person might want. If I had died, I wouldn't want my dad to celebrate *his* birthday one week after.

4

For a week I stayed out of school. Then it was spring vacation, so that was one more week.

My school's called Cobweb by everyone except my dad, who always asked, "How are things at Touchy Feely?" You'd think he'd like my school, because it's into the arts. The brochure says, "We emphasize the arts," and students get music appreciation and art every year, including pottery in the tenth grade, field trips to every museum in New York City, plus matinees at the ballet and the New York Philharmonic. But my dad said, "Your mom should dump you in public school, not namby-pamby land."

"Dad doesn't like Cobweb," I once told her.

She didn't answer but studied an order form. "'If possible, lilacs.' Where am I supposed to get lilacs in winter? Carmen," she called to her assistant, "Did you tell them we'd send lilacs?" My mom owns a flower shop, and that's where we were at the time. She started snipping rose stems. "Your father . . ."

Whenever she says, "your father," as opposed to "your dad," she's having negative thoughts. Opinion, not fact, but opinion based on years of observation, which practically makes it fact. "He's not paying for it," she said at last.

"Why should he if he doesn't like it?"

I've been going to Cobweb since kindergarten. Every week the school holds a meeting, its word for assembly, about world awareness. At the last one a doctor spoke about all the orphans in Africa who had lost their parents to AIDS. The purpose of these meetings is to raise more sensitive human beings, but all that sensitivity didn't stop Sukie Jameson from bragging about her breasts or kids from staring at me when I returned to school.

I stared right back. What I don't want is pity. What I don't want is someone checking me out to see if I'm sad or to see what a person with no dad looks like. Perhaps they expected a mark on my forehead, like an outline of a man with a line through him, kind of like a traffic warning sign.

Jenna was late. I opened my locker and stashed away the books I didn't need, and gave the glares to anyone who looked my way. I wished Jenna had been here early. I wished I wasn't the one waiting. We always share an apple before class— we pass it back and forth—and play the game Where's Waldo?

Waldo is James Albert Fromsky, DDS. We call him Waldo because we're always wondering where he is. We added the DDS to his name because he has big front teeth. I know that doesn't logically follow, but it happened in a fit of giggles at four in the morning after we'd licked an entire package of raw Jell-O off our fingers. Now that he's kissed Jenna, I suppose she knows where he is because he probably calls her on her cell and tells her. I guess it's new stuff all around. Correction: Now that he's kissed Jenna, we both know where he is because, at that very second, he was walking with her to our lockers. They kept bumping into each other accidentally on purpose and laughing about it, until Jenna saw me.

"Frannie, hi."

"Hey," said James.

She took the apple from me, took a bite, and passed it to Waldo James. He sank his big front teeth into it.

"I'll see you at lunch," said James, returning the apple. He headed off down the hall. He has a very unusual way of ambulating. He lopes. His gait resembles that of a wild animal in Africa. Possibly a gazelle.

"Bye-ee," Jenna called to James as she passed the apple to me.

I tossed it in a garbage can that was fortunately nearby.

"Why did you do that?"

I slammed my locker shut and split for class. Jenna may know where Waldo is now, but I intended to lose them both.

"You're going the wrong way," Jenna shouted.

She was right, but I wasn't turning around, no way. I went up to the second floor, took a detour, and came down to the first floor again. As a result, I was late to history, and when I walked in, Denicia Hays, who had cried when the hamsters died in second grade, clapped as though my return to school was something to applaud and everyone else joined in. Dad was right about Cobweb. I should be in public school.

I spent lunch in the chemistry lab. It's always empty during lunch, and if you want privacy, it's the best place to hang. I could hear girls screaming—not like I screamed when I saw my dad, just random shrieks now and then, like a guy had popped a girl's bra strap or put a spider on her neck. Baby stuff.

It was nice in the chemistry lab. It smelled safe, like disinfectant. I ate my tuna sandwich the way I used to, itty bitty bites of crust first, then the soft part after. I wondered what Saran wrap is made of. I decided to read the small type on the box when I got home.

Jenna called that afternoon. "Hi, it's me, where were you?"

"When?"

"I texted you maybe fifty times. At lunch? After school?"

"Busy."

"Oh. So . . ."

"So."

"Frannie?"

"What?"

"Do you want to go to the movies on Saturday? There's a bunch of us going."

"Not really. But thanks anyway." I tossed my cell

phone into the back of my closet. Dad was right—cells are a pain. Instead of talking, you could be looking. Who knows what you're missing? Besides, I didn't need it because there was no one I wanted to talk to.

5

I develop a routine: arriving at school at the very last second, lunch in the chemistry lab, and then directly home, where I mostly lie on the floor and space out on the light, although a huge evergreen outside the window blocks most of it. When I say I'm spacing out on the light, I'm really lying on my back eating chips. No one bothers me, because my mom works her butt off and The Mel commutes to the State University at New Paltz, an hour away. (Sometimes I call him "The Mel" because it sounds beasty, sometimes simply

"Beastoid." With his hulky bod, bizarre hair wave, many freckles that I think of as spots, he definitely qualifies as part creature.)

Even at breakfast Mom is rarely present. At about five A.M. she drives to the flower markets in Poughkeepsie to buy what's fresh. When I was little, I would go with her, and I became expert at predicting which rosebuds would open and which would stay tightly closed until their heads drooped and it was curtains. With roses, the trick isn't cutting them and plunging them (Mom always says "plunge," like it's a submarine, not a stem) into hot water. There's a second sense about whether a flower will blossom, and if you hang around enough of them, eventually you get the gift. Although once they open, there's no telling when they'll die. Sometimes they keep opening bigger and fuller and more and more gloriously. Sometimes a rose looks young and fresh and perky when you go to sleep, and the next morning the blossom flops like its neck's been broken.

For two weeks Jenna calls every night. Mom gives me the messages, but I ignore them. Finally I suppose that her mom called my mom, because my mom comes into my room, sits on the edge of my bed while I'm considering whether to sleep, and says, "I hear you're not seeing Jenna much."

I just shrug.

"You guys have been friends forever, Frannie."

"Things change."

She rubs my foot through the blanket. "Do you want to talk about your dad?"

What does one have to do with the other? "No."

"I'm sorry. I'm so sorry, sweetheart."

She's not sorry, not deep down. I pull the covers up so only my eyes are showing.

Whenever my parents came face-to-face, I watched them carefully. Like when Mom and I bumped into Dad on Warren Street. "Hello, Sean," she said.

I looked to see if she was smiling, but she wasn't.

She was opaque, which, if you look it up in the dictionary, means "impenetrable by light." You wouldn't have a clue from looking at her what she was feeling.

"Where are you guys headed?" asked my dad. He never said her name, Laura.

"Liberty Diner," I said. "Want to come?"

"No thanks."

"He's on his way to the hardware store," said my mom.

"As a matter of fact, I am."

"How'd you know Dad was going to the hardware store?" I asked her while I ate my favorite sandwich, BLT, minus the T, on white toast with mayo.

She said, "Some things never change." That was a negative remark. Here's the deal. They were frenemies. Public friends, private enemies. Now that he's gone, how miserable could she be?

The night after Mom's attempt at sympathy, both she and Mel show up. He sits in my desk chair and polishes his glasses. She perches on the bed again.

"Don't think you're going to be my father," I tell Mel.

"Good grief." He gets up and leaves the room. One down. Maybe they'll have a fight about me later.

"Your dad left you everything, Frannie."

I'm watching *This Old House* on my own personal TV. *This Old House* was my dad's favorite show. They're framing a porch. My mom picks up the remote and hits the mute button.

"We should go over there. When is school out for the summer?"

"Next Wednesday."

"Saturday then. I'll take off work. You should take what you want to keep, and we'll pack up the rest for Goodwill, okay, sweetheart?"

6

On Saturday I wake up with my head throbbing and have to keep a pillow over it. "I have a migraine," I tell Mom.

"That's something new. How do you know about migraines?"

Who doesn't know about migraines? When Jenna's mom (aka BlueBerry) gets them, she lies on the couch, closes the blinds, and puts an icepack on her forehead, and everyone tiptoes. The slightest noise sends stabs of pain down her neck.

"I have pain shooting down my neck."

Mom gently removes the pillow, tilts my head forward, and presses her fingers into the back of my neck. She rubs around and around. It feels fabulous. "That hurts and it's not helping."

She leaves and returns with two Advils and a bowl of yogurt with honey.

"I can't swallow pills."

"I know. That's why I'm putting them in yogurt."

"Don't mash them."

"I won't mash them." She taps the pills into a spoonful of yogurt. "Come on, I swear this will work. Let the yogurt slide down your throat. I heard about this on talk radio."

I am forced to follow her instructions, and the technique works. Thus ends a lifetime of near choking.

An hour later Mom and I are pulling up to Dad's.

The house looks the same, as sturdy as ever. I can't tell you how strange that is. I expect it to be crying. A crying house. Not really, or maybe really.

What I mean is I expected evidence. Not crying, but drooping.

The small one-story house was built two hundred years ago. It has wide weathered shingles and a narrow front porch supported by plain posts. There used to be two small windows, one on either side of the door, but my dad removed them and cut bigger ones. He framed them in wood he'd scavenged from an old barn. The window wood, grayish, did not match the house wood, more brownish. "We're not into matching, are we?" Dad even found old glass for the new windows. For reasons I can't explain, thanks to this old glass, flat reflections appeared to have texture and depth, like ripples and pleats. "Just an illusion," Dad pointed out, "but life is an illusion."

Why is life an illusion?

I have to think about that, because frankly that is one thing he said that I don't get.

Two birch trees tower over the house. We called them the twins. Elegant with white trunks, they're lean, spare in the branches department, and tend to bend and sway. A lilac bush grows right out from under the porch. "An act of will if I've ever seen one," said my dad. Judging from the scads of petals strewn about, it bloomed this spring. Out of respect, it shouldn't have produced a single blossom.

Dad didn't like grass. He planted curly moss instead. No upkeep. As a result, he was not popular on Rosewood Avenue, because everyone else's lawns look like golfing greens. "How long you keeping that stuff, Sean?" "Still like it?" "Aren't you getting sick of it?" Mr. Kinokan, two doors away, never shut up about Dad's moss. "He's stuck on the moss," my dad used to laugh. "What's Mr. Hate Moss going to say today?" I would whisper when we happened to be outside at the same time he was. I guess Mr. Kinokan has high hopes now that there will be a new owner, perhaps another enemy of originality. I mention new owner because the shock when we drive up is a FOR SALE sign.

We sit in the car for a second looking at it.

"Who put it up for sale?"

"Your dad's lawyer. Whatever it brings is yours. We're going to put the money away for your college education."

"Has he been inside?"

"Who?"

"The lawyer."

"I suppose."

I'm thinking about the white mold and wondering if it has spread. Maybe the mold is taking root like the moss. Moss outside, mold inside. Suppose the mold gets me?

"Come on, Frannie. You'll feel better if we take care of things." Either better or dead from an attack of mold.

When we get to the front door, my mom commences a hunt through her purse. "My God, where is it?"

"What?"

"The key."

To my knowledge my mom has never been in Dad's house, ever. "Who gave you a key?"

"His lawyer."

"Look under that big rock. That's the one I use," I say, but at the very same time, she holds up a key dangling off a miniature wooden pennywhistle. "Here it is."

"Where'd you get that?"

"I just told you, your dad's lawyer."

"But that's Dad's key. That's his key chain. He carved that pennywhistle."

"I assumed that."

"Mom, how did they get Dad's key?"

"Frannie, what's the problem? They didn't steal it. It was probably with his stuff. Like his wallet."

"You mean the police went trolling through the house? Do you have the wallet, too?"

"Yes. I have it at home."

"And you didn't tell me?"

"Frannie, calm down."

"I don't want you to come inside."

"What?"

My mom paces back and forth on my dad's porch.

"I'm sorry, but I don't."

"You want to do this alone?" She drops her purse and presses the fingers of both hands into her forehead. I guess now she's got the migraine.

"Yes, I do."

"You don't want my help?" She moves her hands to her hips and looks every direction but at me. Is help on the way? Is a posse expected? Is Mel going to screech up in his trusty Honda?

"Is it my house or not?"

"Frances Anne, you are a bronco." She always uses my whole name when she is utterly exasperated. "I will leave for two hours. Then I'll see how you're doing. Come on, help me get the cardboard boxes out of the trunk."

She leaves me on the porch with about twenty collapsed cardboard boxes and one of those gigantic tape dispensers, which she demonstrates how to use, assembling one box for me. I have to face Mold World alone.

I am scared. Scared and acting stupid. How could Mom have left me here?

I put the key in the lock and do the trick Dad taught me—pull the door toward me and then turn the key. It clicks. The door swings back and sticks in the usual place, where an old floorboard juts up. I push the door open the rest of the way.

His living room now reminds me of Dr. Glazer's waiting room. Dr. Glazer is my dentist. The magazines are stacked on the trunk in three even piles. Someone has plumped the pillows along the back of the couch and covered the bottom cushion, faded green, with one of Dad's striped blankets, a stack of which, on the floor, used to serve as a kind of reclining spot. The blanket is stretched and tucked tightly, possibly with hospital corners. I'm not familiar with hospital corners, but I've heard about them, and these excessively neat folds have hospital written all over them. His rectangular hooked rug, another street prize, which he always set at an angle, is centered in front of the couch. All the small stuff we collected, displayed on the bookshelf, is spaced evenly in a row, small objects in front. And dusted.

I guess his lawyer brought in a cleaning patrol.

Mess is so comforting. I didn't realize this until now, until I look at Dad's living room with none of his personality left in it.

The shades, rolls of bamboo, are unfurled. Never, in all my time at Dad's, have the shades been down and the light, sun or moon, shut out.

I peek into the kitchen. His chipped tile counter gleams, and to the right of the faucet stand Fantastic, Joy dishwashing detergent, and a sponge. Not my dad's. Whoever cleaned is planning to return and clean again. The place smells arid and artificial. Lemony. I open the cabinets—his dishes are stacked too neatly. I check the utensil drawer, where Dad threw things willy-nilly. Still chaos. What a relief. As for the refrigerator . . . It takes nerve to look inside, but I do. There are no leftovers growing crusty or taking root. All that remains are a few jars, each with a secure lid and long shelf life: mayonnaise, Tabasco, Dijon mustard, ketchup.

If you think I'd want to draw this bunch of jars, you'd be wrong. An open milk carton, a wastebasket with crumpled paper inside—those images suggest life. Carefully organized objects—like a fake arrangement of some apples and a pear—suggest the opposite, which would be D-E-A-T-H.

Except one thing. I might draw the tomato can holding pencils. Pencils sharp. Waiting.

I'm not going into the bathroom. Fortunately the door is closed. No sign of mold seeping out from under it.

The narrow hall leads to our bedrooms, mine so little and cozy that my dad dubbed it "the bird's nest." He built a loft bed, and I climb the ladder to look at the red down comforter and the pillowcases with their covered wagons and cowboys. Too baby-ish for me, but still I want them. I toss the pillows down, pull the comforter off the bed, and then drag it all into the living room.

I venture into Dad's room next.

He didn't believe in bureaus. Well, it might not have been a belief exactly, since he never made any declarations about it, and you may have noticed he was big on declarations. He kept all his clothes on open shelves. He constructed them from the beautiful old barn wood he also used for the window frames. The hardest thing about going through Dad's house is that he made almost everything with his own hands or else found it. He didn't buy his bedroom set and shelves at IKEA, the way Mom did for me when we moved in with Mel. How will I choose what to take? How can I leave anything behind?

The only thing on the wall in his bedroom is a giant corkboard. "This wall belongs to you, Frannie." From top to bottom and side to side, he tacked my artwork galore, some from when I was very small drawing pigs and chickens with crayons or markers. For some reason I was really into pigs and chickens. He also displayed my recent efforts: an open car trunk with bags of groceries inside, a rake abandoned in a pile of autumn leaves, an issue of *Condé Naste Traveler* "All about Italy," open, facedown in bands of bright sunlight.

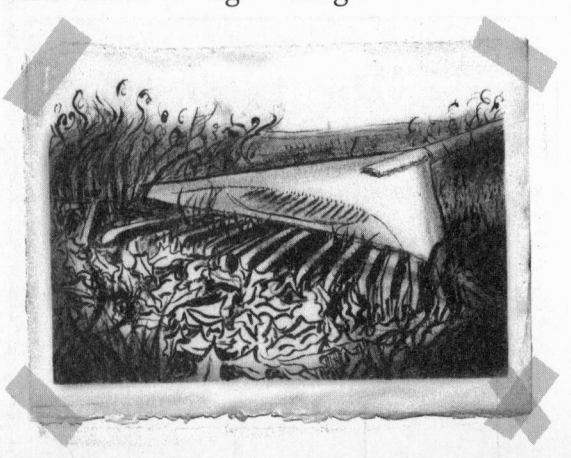

I wonder if Dad ever thought about what he wore, because he kind of had a uniform—a light-blue work shirt worn unbuttoned with the tails hanging out over a T-shirt; black or blue jeans; a brown leather belt about two inches wide with a brass buckle shaped like a star. Sometimes I used his favorite sweater, a light beige pullover, for a blanket while I watched TV. He'd had it forever. When I was younger, like around six years old—right after the divorce, when I was a scaredy-cat about sleeping over at my dad's—he'd light a fire and read to me from my favorite book, *Where the Sidewalk Ends*. He'd be wearing that sweater and his arm was around me. I remember picking at the sleeve.

The sweater lies on top of the shirts, folded carefully, not carelessly the way my dad did it. I pull it over my head. The sleeves dangle below my hands, the V comes down practically to my waist, and the bottom skirts my thighs.

Next to the shelves are my dad's duck-hunting boots. My dad would never hunt a duck, but that's what they're called in the catalogue, and they're useful for tromping in mud. I yank off my shoes and put my feet into the boots.

I assemble a few boxes and pack up the rest of his clothes. I'm keeping them. In a way they're friends. Even though the shirts were identical, I can tell them apart. One has a frayed collar; another, a black ink spot on the pocket; a third, purple stains from being thrown in the washing machine with my red comforter (my mistake). After that, I clomp back into the living room. It isn't easy to walk in his shoes. I have to clench my toes each time I lift my foot to make sure I take the boot with me and don't leave it behind. It's fun actually. Fee fi fo fum. For a second I forget why I'm here.

I put together a bunch more boxes. First I'll pack his clothes, then all the objects we collected. I need newspapers to wrap our treasures securely, so I tromp through the backyard to the big shed. I know where the key to the padlock is, above the window tucked between overlapping shingles. It's a big iron key. I fit it into the heavy old padlock, need both hands to turn it, and the lock releases. I lift off the padlock, turn back the metal flap, and hear the familiar creak as I open the door.

I hit the light switch, and naked bulbs hanging from wires strung across the ceiling light up.

This is where I expect to find Dad. Here in his studio. Wearing his visor to protect his eyes from flying bits of wood. He taught me how to use the jigsaw. Although using it requires extreme concentration, it's not big and awkward like a buzz saw. A buzz saw, in spite of its power, can only go straight, whereas the small jigsaw cuts swirls, curls, curves, and intricate edges. What subtlety, what versatility. My dad could bore you for hours on the gifts of a jigsaw. I heard my mom tell that to Mel. Imagine complaining about Dad's jigsaw rants to Mel, who expounds on Queen Elizabeth and her pomegranate toothpaste. Nevertheless, my mom said it, and, while I'd never tell her, I sort of agree. Jenna does for sure. My dad practically put her to sleep once singing the jigsaw's praises.

Dad must have been sanding the night before he died. The sander is out on his worktable, and the surface is deep in sawdust. Whenever the sander or jigsaw was on, I practically had to scream to get his attention. Then he'd shut it off, flip up the visor, and say, "Hey there, Frannie, what's going on?" Or "Give me five more minutes, baby. Well, maybe ten or twenty."

From the look of things in his woodworking studio, he is just taking a break. His tool drawers are all open, as usual, waiting for his hand to reach in and pull out the exact drill or bit. His metal paint box, also ajar, displays its tiered shelves. There are smears of color everywhere and tubes of acrylics jammed in. Super-giant cans of turpentine and thinner line the wall, as do many empty old wooden picture frames that have no purpose whatsoever. Along the back of his worktable he crammed tin cans containing brushes of all sizes, bristles up. This place is a mess, Dad's mess. He could find anything he needed in an instant.

His very last project lies forsaken on the table—three interlocking pieces of wood with wavy edges. I study it. It looks like something in motion. In Japanese joinery the "joints" are part of the design—you can see them clearly—and the main connection between two of these pieces is triangular, resembling a fin, no, a wing. I pick up the sculpture and swoop it around. The wavy edges seem to slice the air. Dad's bird soars.

I wish this shed could be sealed like a tomb. Just as it is. Preserved forever.

"Listen," he said once, "this is very important." And it is, so you should pay close attention. "If you can make your living with your imagination, that's the best. If you can make it with your hands, that's good too."

Fact, not opinion: My dad did not make much of a living. He sold his work through galleries, one in town, one in the Berkshires, and two on Cape Cod.

One night last fall I heard the frenemies on the phone. Well, I heard my mom's side. "I'd take you to court if it wouldn't upset Frannie."

I waylaid her as soon as she hung up. "Are you mad at Dad?"

"No, honey. We just have issues now and then." Liar.

They were arguing about money. Why else would she take him to court? She had no respect for his life.

I'm going to take this unfinished piece, this wavy bird, although I hate to disturb his studio in any way. By lying here, it lets me believe he'll be back tomorrow. When I get it home and display it on my bookshelf, it will be a relic. If you look up relic in the dictionary, you'll find that all three meanings more or less apply: 1) something that survived from an extinct culture, 2) a memento or keepsake, 3) an object of great regard.

Dad kept bundles of old newspapers around in case he needed to ship his art. Old copies of *The*

New York Times, which he read every single day without fail, are under an old walnut desk in the corner, tucked behind a microwave he never used. I have to get on my hands and knees, and I scrape my arm against the wall doing it. Inspecting, I notice that the whole side of my arm is white. All my insides lurch, my stomach drops into my feet. Mold. Killer mold. I bat at my arm to knock the mold off, and a bit chips off. Dry paint. Not mold. Dry white paint that has rubbed off on me . . . when? A second earlier. The wall I scraped my arm against had been whitewashed. I'd done the whitewashing myself under my dad's supervision. Months before.

I have to calm down because now I'm sweating. I sit on the floor for a while. I'm certain Dad did not whitewash his face before he died, so this paint on my arm and that white on his face have nothing to do with each other. I am really nuts.

I haul out the microwave, and behind it, between it and the newspapers, lies yet another salvaged object, a cardboard suitcase. Whoever heard of a cardboard suitcase? Aha. That's why Dad liked it. It's an object made of something that particular object is not normally made of. You had to know my dad, get into his head, to understand where his thoughts led him. I yank it by the handle. Man, is it heavy. Something shifts inside as I slide it out from under the desk.

The suitcase, banged up, dented in the corners, is splotched with water stains. If Dad had showed it to me, he would have waved it around, pointing out those faded watery blotches against the plain tan background. "Abstract art, Frannie, you think it came out of nowhere?" Once he showed me a photograph of Main Street—a view smack down the middle with stores and a sidewalk on each side. Little by little, he blocked all the images until only the white line down the center of the street remained. "Abstract art," he proclaimed, "is the reduction of the landscape or the scrambling of it. It's been there forever, right in front of our faces, but it took hundreds of years before an artist saw it. Always trust your eyes. They'll lead you where you need to go."

Trust my eyes? I'm not sure what he meant. How do we not trust our eyes? What other way is there to see?

I have to think about that.

My apologies. I'm getting sidetracked. I have to remember everything Dad said, you see, because who else will? I press the buttons on the rusted locks. They release. Even so, the top and bottom refuse to separate.

I find a screwdriver and pry open the top of the suitcase. Inside lies an object about the size of a gigantic dictionary in the school library, those books so mammoth that they have to have their own stands. Tissue paper is folded around it— crackly old tissue faded into uneven shades of pink. As I lift the heavy object, it falls out of the paper and thuds to the floor. I gasp because it is beautiful, and because, in my first encounter, I nearly damaged it.

My birthday present. Not a doubt. I know instantly.

A carved wooden box. The most exquisitely carved wooden box with my name engraved in the center. Not in curlicue letters. My dad hated fairy-tale kind of lettering. He liked it plain. Underneath, it says "1000."

FRANCES ANNE

1000

Never before has my name seemed elegant. For a second I forgive my parents for giving it to me. It isn't the name of my grandmother or great-grandmother or some highly admired friend. There's no excuse for bestowing that dreary tag on me. But carved by my dad's hand, my name has beauty. Even a pleasing lilt when I pronounce it. Which I do right now, very softly. Around it, setting it off to perfection like a lace ruffle around a valentine, he carved a rectangular border of Celtic knots.

My dad was Irish, and all Irish were Celts a thousand years before anyone had a hair dryer. When my dad first mentioned Celtic knots, I thought they were real knots made of rope, but they're not. They're designs found in an ancient Bible called The Book of Kells from 800 A.D. "Loops with no beginning and no end," my dad explained. "Like time or the ocean." It must have taken him ages to carve something this intricate and delicate.

I stroke the honey-colored wood. It feels meltingly soft, as if Jenna has given it one of her super-duper moisturizing treatments.

Considering that this gift is from my dad, it's very wrapped. Fancily wrapped. Usually he used aluminum foil. Occasionally he twisted newspaper around whatever he was giving me. He never sealed anything with Scotch tape or tied it with ribbon. He'd saved this paper for sure. Dad and I recycled everything, while my mom has a bad case of Discardia. That's what he called the tendency to dump perfectly useful things. Here's what's eerie. It wasn't like Dad to plan ahead. When he had to complete art for a show, he always slaved down to the wire. But he finished this before my birthday. Weeks before. Could he have had a premonition that maybe he wouldn't be here?

"Frannie!"

My mom can certainly wreck a moment. She bellows. She could call the cows home, I'm not kidding. What a waste that we live in a place where there are no cows. And her timing is hideous.

I mash newspapers over the box. This is none of her business. "I'm in Dad's studio. I'll be out in a second," I bellow back.

She saunters in anyway. "How's it going?"

"Fine. I was looking for newspaper to wrap up Dad's special artifacts."

"Those things on the bookshelf?"

"I love them."

"I know you do."

She takes a quick look around and heads for

Dad's drafting table. Leaning across it, she studies a watercolor tacked on the wall. I don't know why Dad liked that watercolor, because it wasn't his style. For one thing it was fruit, specifically red and green grapes. How ordinary. For another, it was pretty—well, Dad would probably call it "decorative," with a sneer. That would let you know he had higher standards. Trust Mom to make a beeline for the most conventional. Maybe Dad appreciated the painting because it was on a placemat. At least I think it was a placemat, because the white paper was a rectangle about placemat size with scalloped edges.

"A bunch of grapes," I tell her, because they are smudgy and watery—more impressionistic than realistic and maybe she doesn't get it.

"I know," she says.

"Mom, I left clothes and stuff that I want to take in the living room. Would you be a doll and help me pack them up? I'll be right inside."

That catches her attention. She stops scrutinizing

the grapes and swings around. "'Be a doll'?"

I am so lame. How fake is that? Mom is going to glom right onto this gigantic lump covered in newspapers and drill me about it. "What's going on? What have you got there, Frannie?"

But instead she laughs. "'Be a doll'? I guess I could be a doll." And she leaves. In a second I hear her shoes squishing the wet moss, and then the screen door to the house bangs.

Quickly I empty a smelly old cardboard box containing cans of turpentine. I set my beautiful present inside, protected by several layers of newspaper. I wrap up Dad's work in progress too, the wavy bird, and tuck it inside, then stack some tools around for camouflage: a hammer, screwdriver, electric drill. The box weighs as much as Mambo, Jenna's Labrador retriever. I try not to huff and puff carrying it into the house, but Mom doesn't notice anyway. She's standing next to the CD player listening to Dad's pennywhistle music. The pennywhistle (a little flute a goat herder might play to keep herself amused) sounds like birds dizzily twittering back and forth. Everyone says birds sing, but in my opinion they don't. They just make the same few chirps over and over again. The pennywhistle is the birdsong of your imagination—if birds really could jump on a tune and run with it. It's major Irish, hence Dad's infatuation. And it must have been on his CD player, so I guess Mom just punched the thing for music to keep her company. She doesn't hear me walk right past—undoubtedly because she's trying to think of something nasty to say about the music, it being another of Dad's eccentricities. I'm able to lug the box through the living room and out to the car without her paying the least attention. When I return, she's still in the same place, her foot thumping in irritation.

She stops mid thump, her shoulders jerk in surprise. "Oh, hi, Frannie."

Who else were you expecting?

She begins thumbing through Dad's CDs. "Where were you?"

"Putting a box in the trunk. What are you looking for?"

"Huh?"

She's acting weird. She's acting like someone I know. Who? Me. She's acting the way I do when I'm feeling guilty—slightly unglued. I look closely to make sure she isn't pocketing something of Dad's that she doesn't want me to have. "I'm packing," she adds.

Only of course she isn't.

Mom hits the button, silencing the birdsong. "So?"

"So?"

She grabs the tape dispenser, karate chops a collapsed box to open it up, seals the seams in two shakes, and begins packing up Dad's clothes.

7

Having that secret present makes it much easier to leave Dad's. I try not to pay too much attention to the ransacked quality of the house. Nor do I want to consider the irony: Some leftovers might end up in the dump, right where they came from.

"You can come back again," Mom tells me.

"I know. I'll come whenever I want."

"Until it's sold."

Thank you for the reminder.

"We should store everything in the garage," she

says as we pull into the driveway. "There are at least twelve boxes."

"No, in my room. I want them with me." I fake a little catch in my throat, although here's a warning: Working up to a crying fit, even as a big fat act, is like being in a rowboat on top of Niagara Falls. Pretty hard to change direction.

"All right, fine," my mom says, as I blow my nose on a tissue she provides. "Whatever you want."

Wow. Me have power. I think she might be scared of upsetting me.

Cardboard could not possibly absorb oxygen (or emit carbon monoxide). Impossible, right? But no question my room smells stale now that it's a storage facility. Breathing ceases to be a pleasant activity. I move four cartons down to the garage. Strategically, I believe it makes my mom less likely to hound me. Practically, I believe it ups my odds of survival.

I have to wait until ten at night to look inside my beautiful carved box. Ten is when Mom and Mel turn into pumpkins. Most likely it's a jewelry box. Little compartments. An upper shelf that lifts out. But what about that 1000?

FRANCES ANNE
1000

What does it mean? Obviously not my age. Could it be a year? Doubtful. A lucky number? Dad never mentioned a lucky number. How about a mystery number—something he expects me to spend the rest of my life puzzling over? My dad was a bit twisted—imagine liking crazy bird music—but he wasn't that twisted. Could it be something inside the box? Maybe a check for a thousand dollars that my mom will force me to put away for college. No way. Dad never gave money for presents. One thousand . . . let's see. One thousand balloons that I have to blow up myself? That's more likely. One thousand pearls. Get real, Frannie. One thousand wildflower seeds. A bit tedious to count them, don't you think, although Dad and I do love wildflowers.

As soon as the light blinks out under Mom and Mel's door, I dig the box out of its camouflage. I carry it to the windowseat, my favorite place to cuddle up, and ease off the top. At first look the contents seriously underwhelm. Flat pieces of wood. Not to get too negative, but the box is jam-packed, every inch, with bits I might sweep off his studio floor.

My dad wouldn't spend months carving something gorgeous, then use it for a wastebasket. That makes no sense.

Just when I'm beginning to get grumpy, the box catches a beam of moonlight and shines in its very own pool of white light, illuminating dots and splashes of color. I grasp a handful of wooden bits. Each, about the size of a postage stamp, is painted and its edges have tiny knobs and notches—little fingers poking in and out. I feel ridges along the cut edges, the roughness of the paint. A handmade jigsaw puzzle. Dad painted and cut every piece.

There have to be hundreds of pieces here.

My heart is racing. I feel jittery, as if I might topple over.

I've done puzzles. At Jenna's. Her family does a giant puzzle every Christmas. The hardest one they ever did was called New England Fall. From participating, I knew that you should always begin with the border. Then do sections, preferably buildings or animals—solid, clear, identifiable objects. That's why New England Fall was such a nightmare—it was all trees with masses and masses of leaves. "Don't go near the blues until the end," her dad would say over and over, and Jenna would groan, "We know that, Daddy." Blues mean sky or water, the hardest part of any puzzle.

Digging into the box, letting the pieces fall between my fingers, I collect all the ones with straight edges. Over and over, I plow through. Ouch. A paper cut. I put my finger in my mouth and suck it, which causes me to raise my head. From spending hours in a weird bent-over position, my neck makes crinkly sounds, as if a paper bag was stuffed inside. I hope my vertebrae aren't disintegrating. By now my eyes ache and I'm loopy from concentrating so hard. Perhaps that's why it takes me a good ten minutes to realize that, if I got a paper cut, there must be paper.

A birthday card? A note from Dad?

I leap up, or try to, but my legs are nearly paralyzed from not moving for hours. Man, doing puzzles is a bitch; you have to stretch and massage to recover from it. I do not have a proper puzzle work space, that's for sure. Carefully I move the border pieces in neat piles to the top of my bureau, then dump out the remainder of the box onto the bed. The pieces tumble out in a pile, and a photo slides out with them.

A four-by-six snapshot of somewhere ancient by the sea.

A village nestled around a cove at the base of a hillside. The houses, three and four stories tall, all have green shutters and tile roofs, but are painted a variety of colors. I know a lot about paint, thanks to Dad, and even in a photograph where color gets distorted, I can tell that the sun tortured these colors, stripping them of vibrancy but leaving something lovelier. There are bleached-out pinks of every hue, colors faded to white but exuding whiffs of peach or lime. Some buildings have horizontal stripes, yellow or white bands below the windows on each floor, which is kind of nutty, at least nothing I've ever seen before. It makes me think that this village is a cheerful place. Beyond the town, near the top of the hill or small mountain, there's a block of green (a garden or woods?), and next to that something orange (a structure?). In this small snapshot, the details are unclear. Along the right side, stone steps lead up the mountain. The cove has a shallow shore, a little outdoor café with brightly colored patio umbrellas, and at the far end a gray stone church.

I'm going to draw the photo for you. A lifetime

of celebrating mundane moments, such as an empty ketchup bottle next to some half-eaten French fries, did not prepare me for landscapes, but here's my best shot.

Here's what I think. This is not the United States. Here's why. No motorboats.

Cape Cod's a very old place for the United States. I went there to see my dad's show. While Dad and I ate lobster rolls on the beach (which had pale, soft, pillowy sand and giant dunes, nothing like that narrow, flat brown beach in the photo), he told me that Cape Cod wasn't half as beautiful or old as the country where his grandparents were born.

According to Dad, there are sleepy seaside towns in Ireland where nothing has changed for centuries. The village in this photo has no motor boats; it looks like it might not even have televisions, telephones, or cars. If there were cars, on what would they travel? I see neither a road, nor a driveway, nor a garage. Examining this photo—trust your eyes, remember—I have the distinct impression that these houses crowded together are survivors. They are so picturesque as to be from another time.

The place must still exist, because the photo isn't old. It's indistinguishable from any small snapshot that you get back from a local one-hour photo lab where the clerk asks, "Glossy or matte?" This is glossy. "Border or no?" This has a border.

The photo is a miniature replica of this puzzle. It has to be. Why else is it in the box? It all adds up, doesn't it? It's impossible for anyone to do a gazillion-piece puzzle without some idea of what it is. Dad had to know that. He wouldn't set an impossible task. What kind of birthday present would that be? Ireland is the home of my long-demised great-granny and -gramps. I bet this is the very village they grew up in. A piece of my past. My past in pieces.

I rest there thinking about Dad for quite a while. Over the last weeks I have tried to conjure him up a few times, vegging in my bedroom in the afternoons. If I lie still, without moving so much as an eyelash, maybe I'll feel his energy floating around me, above me. Somewhere. But nothing. I despair that I'm not the spiritual type. But this puzzle makes him feel closer. It's here for a reason, it must be. Something sacred, a secret just between us. Once I put it together, I'll know.

8

The next day is Sunday.

On Sundays Mom and Mel are home. As usual she's stretched out on the couch doing the cross-word, while he's parked in the modern metal-and-leather armchair with stacks of papers around his feet.

They always sit in the same places. Mel owns the chair, Mom owns the couch. It's like they have assigned seating.

I need to get to Kinko's all by myself.

I also need to sneak a big board into the house.

Here's what I realize about my life. When Mom and Mel are home, I have only the illusion of privacy. Life may be an illusion, as Dad says. I have no idea. For me, privacy is an illusion for sure.

Consider: Being able to close your door and post a threatening KEEP OUT note does not constitute privacy. All kids slap KEEP OUT signs on their doors, and it is my suspicion that parents think it's cute, even adorable. My definition of adorable: a bunny rabbit. I do not want to be thought of as bunny-rabbit-like. Might as well pin a pom-pom on my butt. As for the K-O sign, who respects it, really? If your door has no lock, you might as well add *please*, as in KEEP OUT PLEASE, and pray for respect. Furthermore, in a town like this, where the main drag is two miles from the house and the nearest mini mall with a Kinko's is three, you have to be carted around before you can drive. I am fifteen years old, too young for a driver's license, too old for a bicycle. I exist at the mercy of others.

Yes. Privacy is an illusion.

"I'm really tired," I tell Mom and Mel.

It's true, I'm beat. I hunted for border pieces until four A.M., and fell asleep by accident. When I woke up, a puzzle piece was pressed into my cheek, leaving an indentation. I had to rub my cheek with lotion. All I could find was Neutrogena oil-free sunblock with 30 percent protection. *Not to be swallowed*, according to the fine print on the bottle. *Avoid contact with eyes*. I still have a dent in my cheek, but not a crater, and nothing shaped like something that indicated that my cheek should be interlocked with some other cheek.

"Come over, let me kiss your forehead."

Mom has this unique way of taking temperature with a kiss.

"I'm fine, I'm just tired. I'm going to sleep."

Mom and Mel exchange a quick look. "You slept until noon."

"I know, but I didn't sleep well. There was an opossum outside the window."

I retreat to my room, close the door, and lie on the floor, flat on my back—I don't know why I like to do this so much. It's a little easier to feel that you're nowhere. After getting bored, I wiggle over to the bed, flip over, and pull out my present. Hard to be separated from it for long. By now I've collected a bunch of border pieces and stashed them in a shoe box. I begin the search for more.

"Frannie."

The door flies open. I shove my present under the bed. "What, Mom?"

"You're lying on the floor."

"I'm sleeping."

"On the floor?"

"You woke me. What is it?" She is so getting on my nerves.

"You need a summer job."

"What?" I sit up.

"You can't sleep all day. It's not healthy."

"I won't work."

"You have to."

"What, you're going to make me? Try it. I'm not leaving this room."

"Frances, you cannot lie on the floor while Mel and I go to work."

"I like the floor."

"You were sleeping."

"No, I wasn't."

"Didn't you say you were?"

"No." A lie.

"You said you were going to your room to sleep and now I find you on the floor. What's that?"

"Why?"

This is a great trick. I highly recommend it. Sidetrack them with something nonresponsive. She says, "What's that?" I respond, "Why?" This gets the parent very confused. She freezes, trying to remember what she said one second earlier that would make you say what you said, and that little freeze gives you an edge.

"I want to go to Kinko's."

"Who's Kinko?"

See, she's spinning. "The copy place. I want to copy some photos of Dad."

Anything to do with Dad she agrees to. "Oh, sure. I guess so. In an hour."

9

Mom's delivery van is usually refreshingly cool because it's refrigerated, but when there are no flowers to keep fresh, she switches off the air-conditioning. As a result, on this muggy June day my thighs stick together and to the seat. Mom named her shop after me, Frannie's Flowers. I was five at the time (right after the divorce); I suppose I was flattered. Now I find it a tad embarrassing. Perhaps I wouldn't mind so much if the lettering on the van (and on the shop window, the stationery, and the website) wasn't so adorable: swirly turquoise letters frosted with lime curlicues. I remember once telling Dad, "Cover your eyes, Mom's van is headed this way."

He laughed, and gave me a squeeze. When Dad squeezed, I lifted off the ground. Or did I? As I remember it, when he swung his arm around my shoulder and pulled me to him, for the tiniest split second, earth seemed unnecessary.

I have begun to worry about how quickly memories evaporate. I don't mean what Dad looks like, but the sensation of being with him. Whenever I made Dad laugh, I felt proud. These feelings—his laughter and the swelling of my chest in happiness—went together. I know it. I can tell you that. But feeling it is over. My possibilities for experiencing happiness have contracted. Fact, not opinion. Will they shrink more and more?

"You don't have to come inside with me," I tell Mom.

"Oh. I'm not allowed?"

Good grief. I didn't say that, did I? That she's

not allowed? My mom is witchy. She leaps from what you say to what you mean. Another invasion of privacy. "This van smells like the inside of a vase," I say.

"What are you talking about?"

She starts sniffing, and, while she's trying to detect foul odor, I escape to Kinko's.

I brought two snapshots of my dad—if Mom asked what I was enlarging, I could show her those—and the photo from the box, the real reason for the Kinko's trip.

Once Dad and I saw this foreign film *Blow-Up*, about a photographer who kept enlarging a photo. At first look, in mini size, the image was innocuous, a woodsy park full of bountiful leafy trees. A ton of magnifications later, he saw a gun poking out between some branches, then, in the underbrush, a body.

If I blow this puzzle picture up, will there be a shotgun angled through one of the shuttered windows? Will a lady be crouched behind a boat? Will there be mysterious shadows? The actual puzzle will be much bigger than this small snapshot. I don't want to be surprised when I put it together. I used to like surprises, but after finding my dad dead, I'm surprised out.

The fellow behind the counter upends the envelope and shakes out three photos. "How large can you make these?" I ask.

He points to the photos of Dad. "These I can do as big as you want. But this"—he indicates the puzzle snapshot—"is dinky."

"Dinky?"

"Weak resolution."

"What's that?"

"The quality is poor. Can't go much bigger than eight by ten."

"That's all? Eight by ten? Okay. Do them all eight by ten. Color Xerox, please."

He walks over to the machine, flips up the cover, positions one photo on the glass, and lowers the cover back down over it.

Why is that cover made of thick rubber? Do we need protection from Xerox rays? Is it like an X-ray machine?

There's no air in here. Gigantic panes of glass, but no functioning windows. The rays could collect. Concentrate. My arms feel twitchy. Am I imagining it? My legs feel twitchy too. "I'll wait outside," I tell the guy, and using my shirt to grasp the knob, I open the door and step outside.

Should I ask my mom to drive me to the emergency room? I am definitely twitchy. Her van is parked three lanes over and toward the back. She can't see me loitering about in a twitchy state. My scalp itches.

"Hey there, Frannie."

A car rolls by. James Albert Fromsky is hanging out the window like a beach towel out to dry. The car makes a right turn out of the parking lot. He's gone before I have time to insult him. What's his story? Why is he so fresh that he can fling out a hi-de-ho? He barely knows me. Must be because of Jenna. They probably IM'ed fifty times last night.

"Hey, miss." The Kinko's guy beckons me inside.

He lays a photo on the counter: Dad grinning his great wall-to-wall smile as he waves his chopsticks. In this blowup I can see all the friendly crinkles around his eyes. He's carrying on about something. Probably what a perfect container Chinese food arrives in. He loved those white boxes. He said, "A perfect thing cannot be improved on." Dad also said that I was a perfect thing.

Forgot that.

I barely register the second eight by ten, of Dad's face hidden behind the visor and goggles. Larger, yes, but no riveting revelation: the brand name ArtWear on the nose guard, flecks of yellow sawdust in Dad's black hair. I'm musing on perfect me with my bumpy nose, long face, hedge hair, although excellent legs, and bad mood.

"Weird," he says, "I tried it three times."

"What?"

He lays down the third enlargement—no image at all, just blotches of color all run together.

"What's this?"

"Your snapshot." His tongue is pierced, and when he speaks a little silver ball bobbles up and down.

"But a Xerox is a photocopy. The color can't run. It's not like it's water or paint or tears." I touch it. It looks wet but it's not.

"Maybe it's got a scrambler?"

"What's that?"

He chuckles without opening his mouth. Actually it sounds more like his stomach is rumbling. "I made it up. You know, like in sci-fi, something embedded in the photo that makes it impossible to copy. Woo, woo, woo."

Right. I really have time for this. "Please try it again."

He fishes two crumpled copies out of the trash and flattens them. "I tried it a bunch of times. Same deal."

"This is impossible."

"I said it was weird. I won't charge you."

"But I need it bigger. I can barely see what's there."

"Sorry."

"Where's the original?"

He looks around, pats the counter, checks the floor.

"Are you almost done?" Mom trills over my shoulder just as Kinko's man from outer space remembers he put all the originals back in my envelope and left it on the machine. "Nice pictures of your dad," she comments about the enlargements. "What's this?" She scrutinizes the watery image.

"An abstract painting Dad did. Do you need any paper, Mom, they have a special, five hundred sheets for three dollars, or what about this, they make stamps with inkpads, maybe you could get a stamp for your store?"

With aimless chatter I manage to keep her

occupied (and the Kinko's fellow confined to saying, "Here's your change") while I double-check the envelope. The original puzzle snapshot is inside, thank goodness, intact.

As we leave, Mom whispers, "Don't ever do that."

"What?"

"Pierce your tongue. I could not survive that, Frannie."

10

That night, after Mom and Mel fall asleep, I sneak out to the garage.

A dirty old bookcase, an el-cheapo model, has been shoved behind some bicycles. I clear space around it, dust it off, unscrew the back, and lay the board on the floor. On an old desk chair Mom has stacked clay pots. I remove them, flip the chair over, and unscrew the casters. The whole time I'm working, I send thanks to my dad, who was the world's handiest. He taught me to be fearless around tools. I was like the surgeon's assistant.

"Phillips head," he would say, and I would hand over the proper screwdriver. "Pliers, balance, epoxy, hammer." I prided myself on a quick response. Then he would step back, "You can finish up," and I would take over, smacking the nails flush to the wood, sanding to the smoothest finish, turning the screws a final few times. With all that experience I had no trouble fastening the casters to the board, one in each corner.

I'm guessing about the size of the puzzle once it's completed, but I'm pretty certain this board is bigger. I can work the puzzle on it. At the same time the board, about my height, is smaller than a twin bed. I can roll it under my bed, out of sight.

The bigger problem is carrying the board into the house without waking Mom or The Mel.

I roll the board out of the garage, down the driveway, and around to the kitchen door. Now the tricky part, lugging it through the house and up to my room. I tilt the board so it stands, grab each side, and lift. To my surprise, it isn't heavy. The wheels might weigh more than the board. I bet it's not solid wood but two pieces of laminate with something in between like plastic. Mom probably can't tell real wood from fake. She doesn't know anything about wood. She probably doesn't even know what grain is, and I don't mean wheat.

The wheels bang into the wall when I carry the board through the doorway from the dining room to the hall. No sound of stirring from above. I whack the board again on the stairs. Not even a hiccup from Mom's room. I could have robbed the place bare.

In my room I lower the board to the floor and slide it under the bed. It rolls exquisitely and fits perfectly.

I pull it out. I shove it back. Out, back, out, back. Out.

I organize the border pieces on the board by color, paying acute attention to subtle distinctions. These bubblegummy pinks go together, but not these soft baby ones. This piece is too mustardy to lump with sunshine yellow, this green is too olive to bond with sage. I bet Dad knew that putting together a puzzle is the all-time sensitize-yourself-to-color experience—wallow in its variety, train the eyeballs to appreciate shadings and tone. This little knobby bit looks like it fits perfectly into this indentation. It snaps in. My first two border pieces lock together—what a rush. I check the clock. It's one in the morning. One more match-up and then I'll go to sleep.

Two hours and twelve matches later, I am still declaring, *One more, and then I'll stop*. It's so utterly absorbing, and you know what else? While I work the puzzle, my mind is peaceful instead of jumpy and full of wretched worries.

Did Dad know this, too? Did he have a premonition that I would need calming down?

11

In the morning I push the eight cardboard storage boxes against the wall. I need space to roll out the puzzle board, plus enough extra area for the wooden box. The box lid, inside up, holds the border pieces that I cull from all the jigsaw pieces in the box bottom. My bureau is partially blocked. I can reach my underwear drawer (the top one) by climbing over the boxes and can get into my closet by edging sideways. This turns out to be fine, not because I decide to spend all day in my bra and undies, but because of this thing I discover: I'm happier in Dad's clothes. And would I have any idea of this if the route were direct? No.

I was contorting around a box to get to my T-shirts when I noticed, bulging out between the cardboard flaps, a bit of blue fabric: one of his shirts. It was there, accessible, easy, so I put it on. The shirt, limp from many washings, felt especially soft on my skin. Digging farther into the box, I unearthed his old beige sweater and layered it over. They are both so huge that, while I'm wearing them, I can pull right out of the sleeves and wrap my arms around my naked body. The clothes double as a tent. I assume tent pose whenever I take a break from working the puzzle, which is almost never.

When I extracted his shirt, his baseball cap flew out too. Dad was a Yankees fan—the cap is black with NY in white lettering. It fits just fine. I can even pull my hair through the hole in the back.

Dad's jeans would have fallen off me—too bad. I have to wear my own, which are lying where I always leave them, on the bathroom floor.

When I arrive in the kitchen, around eight thirty, Mel is puttering. I putter past, grab the Cheerios box and a few more supplies to keep me fortified: raisins, orange soda, and a jar of peanut butter that I like to eat off my fingers. I've got Mel trained. He's used to my not talking, but this morning I act tired and make a lot of noise yawning so he doesn't dare to tell me what serfs ate for breakfast. This summer he's writing a book about serfs, who were slaves in the Middle Ages. You don't want to say the word *serf* around him. Not that it would ever come up, but you don't even want to say the word Nerf, as in Nerf ball, because he might say, "You know what Nerf rhymes with? Serf." And he'll be off and running with arcane facts about serfs, like how they had no napkins.

Mel won't bother me because 1) of the aforementioned training, and 2) once he makes a pot of coffee and transfers it to a thermos, he retreats to his office and doesn't emerge until Mom comes home.

I'm able to work the puzzle all day and the next.

At dinner Mom complains. "I called you, Frannie—why didn't you answer?"

"I got rid of my cell phone. I don't want one, and I don't go anywhere, so don't tell me you have to be able to find me."

If you want to freak a parent out, tell them you don't want your cell phone. If you want them to fall off their chairs in a dead faint, that's the way to do it. The color drains from Mom's face. She looks positively wobbly.

"What were you calling about?" I ask as I struggle to cut a lamb chop with a plastic knife.

She doesn't answer. I glance up again, still busy sawing. She and Mel are transfixed by my struggle. Transfixed (you know what it means, but for emphasis I'll remind you: to render motionless as with terror). I pretend not to notice. "What did you want?"

"Nothing. Just to see how you were."

I reach for some ketchup, and Dad's billowy shirtsleeve lands on the spinach. "Oops."

Mom and Mel appear gripped by that, too. Here's what else I notice: As we continue eating, all you can hear are knives and forks scraping plates. Qualification: Since my utensils are plastic, you can't hear them. You can hear only Mom's and Mel's. Still, I guess we're having a movie moment.

The next day I finish the border, an awesome thing, and measure the puzzle: thirty by twenty-one inches.

After stowing everything under the bed, I attempt to straighten up. My joints pop and creak. It's necessary to shake out my limbs before descending the stairs.

I poke around in the refrigerator: coleslaw, yogurt, tortillas. Boring. Rummage through the crisper. Would you ever want to snack on celery? Isn't that the definition of desperation? What's this? Sliced ham, practically vacuum sealed. That's another way the frenemies were opposite: food storage. I unpeel the Saran wrap and, before eating, fold a ham slice into quarters. While chewing, I begin to wonder about Saran wrap. I read the writing on the box. *The film in Saran Premium Wrap does not contain chlorine.* That's good, I guess, but what film? No indication of what this plastic wrap actually is, just what it isn't. No warnings like *Do not wrap food with this for more than a week.* That would be typical. Wrap less than a week, keeps fresh; wrap more than a week, kills you. But apparently not. Safe to swallow, so I do. Peel the fat off another piece, tilt my head back, and drop it in my mouth.

"Sean!"

"Dad?" I whirl around.

My mom, outside, gapes at me through the kitchen window. Ever heard the expression "jaw-dropping"? Well, Mom's jaw was on the driveway right next to the car wheels. "My God," she says. "I thought you were Sean."

"Me?"

She opens the back door and totters in.

"The clothes, the hat. I don't know, I thought . . ."

She dumps her grocery bag on the table and sinks into a chair.

I see him again at that moment, crumpled on the floor, one leg in one direction, one in the other. Startled. Mold on his face.

"We have to take those clothes to Goodwill. Pack them up."

"I'm wearing them."

"Exactly my point."

"I was wearing them yesterday and the day before. It's not my fault that you're out of control. These are mine, he was mine. You got rid of him."

"Frances Anne, this is out of hand!"

"You mistook me for a dead man."

I don't wait to see her reaction. I hope her jaw hits the floor and stays there. I hope her eyes pop out and bounce off the walls like pinballs. They're no good to her anyway, because she surely can't trust them.

For one second I believed he was alive again. Furthermore, thanks to her, I referred to Dad as a dead man. Like that's all he is.

On my way upstairs, I pass Mel. "Is your mother okay? Honey," he calls, "are you all right?"

I lean over the banister to watch their reunion. Mom is still collapsed in the kitchen chair. She tilts up her head for a kiss. "Hi, Booper."

12

"Wake up, Frannie."

Mashing my face into the bed, I utter agonized throaty moans.

"Frannie."

She shakes my shoulder.

My head feels like lead, it has to be four in the morning. No, four in the morning was when I went to sleep. "What time is it?"

"Seven. You're going to work."

My eyelids refuse to obey signals from my brain,

but I manage to prop myself up on my elbows. "What?"

"You're going to work."

Now I can see her—this whirlybird hauling boxes away from the bureau, opening drawers, flinging a T-shirt, bra, and underpants onto the bed. "Hey, watch out," I shout, because she nearly bangs the shelf where I have artfully displayed Dad's beloved objects: the wavy bird and all the dump treasures. "I won't work in your flower shop. I hate flowers."

At that moment her cell phone rings, and in the middle of forcing me out of bed into work slash jail, Mom snaps instructions to Carmen at the flower market. "Three dozen in apricot. Six flats of pansies. Same with ranunculus and petunias. Assorted." She opens my closet and tosses my Nikes on the bed.

I lie back down.

"Lilies? Let's see, yellow and white. You pick the roses, whatever looks good. Thank you, Carmen." She yanks the blankets off me. "I mean it, Frannie. Up."

"No." I pull the blankets over my head.

Suddenly the bed sags, so I guess she's sitting on it.

I flop the covers down. "I don't want to go to work with you. If I do, I'll just sit there, and if the phone rings, I'll tell them, I don't know what, you're closed or something. I'll make them hang up." I have to stay here. I have to do this thing that Dad left for me, but I can't tell her that. I won't tell her. It's not her business. It's mine. I'm going to do the puzzle today and every day until it's finished.

My mom taps the phone against the bedstead. She stares at the wall as if she's never before seen my amazing Paul Klee poster of *Dream City*. Her silence gives me the creeps. All I hear is a leaf blower blasting, but far away down the block. I'm not breaking the silence. I'm not working at her stupid store, either.

"Not at the store," she says finally.

What is she talking about? She's tricking me to get me to talk, and if I talk to her, she thinks she can talk me into something.

She goes to the bureau and takes a tissue from the box. In the mirror, oh God, not really, I see her blot her eyes and blow her nose. She's crying. My mom is crying. "I don't know what to do for you," she says. Her shoulders shake and little piglike noises squeak out, I guess from trying not to cry and failing.

I have never seen my mom lose it. Not even when the oven didn't light, and, like an idiot, she looked inside—did Hansel and Gretel teach her nothing? *Whoosh*, the oven fired up, singed her, and for a month she walked around with no bangs or eyebrows, looking like an egg.

An hour later, I am on a yellow school bus. I'm the oldest person, the only teenager. Everyone else is between the ages of five and ten. I have my lunch in a brown bag. Fact, not opinion: If your mom cries, she can get you to do anything.

13

"You have to ride with the campers," Mom tells me as a final zetz. A zetz is a zap spiked with extra nasty. "I have to go to work."

Mr. DeAngelo, the driver, invites me to "sit wherever," so I collapse in the first available seat, which happens to be right behind him, after a quick alarming glance at the maniacs farther back. Kids bounce up and down, scream, snatch things. One boy dives over a seat back and ends up with his legs poking into the air.

Mr. DeAngelo pulls the bus over. "Rocco, get your ass in the seat."

I don't think Mr. DeAngelo is supposed to use the word *ass* when addressing the kids. Rocco's legs fall sideways, causing another kid, not visible, to howl—presumably Rocco's legs have clubbed him. A second later Rocco's head bobs up. He has a pudgy face, cheeks like fat peaches, and enormous round black eyes. I had a stuffed dog once with exactly the same eyes, only the dog's eyes were made of felt. "You're holding up the bus." Mr. DeAngelo talks to him without turning around. He observes him in the rearview mirror.

"Sit down, dodo." A girl with pigtails yanks Rocco's arm, and he plops down out of sight. Now, I assume, he's sitting. I also assume, because she used the term *dodo*, that the girl is his sister.

"You can keep driving now, Mr. DeAngelo," she says.

"Thank you, Lark."

As the bus continues on, the kid behind me kicks my seat.

I will never forgive my mother for this. Never, as long as I live.

"Why don't you teach them a song?" Mr. DeAngelo is addressing me via his rearview mirror.

I should teach them a song? How astonishing. Maybe he'll forget he said it.

"Aren't you a counselor?"

"Yes."

"Teach them a song. They like that."

"I don't know any." I close my eyes. Maybe I can nap. Another kick. I swing around. "Don't kick the seat."

Two little girls clutching Barbie dolls cease all motion. "Sorry," one whispers. "I didn't mean to," says the other barely audibly, and she sticks her thumb in her mouth. Good grief. I've made her revert to infancy. I should have been nice. I should have asked, "Is that Malibu Barbie? I see she has a surf board and is dressed for the beach." Or at the very least, "What's your doll's name?" Although aren't all Barbies named Barbie? I don't know—I was never a doll person.

The bus rumbles along out of Hudson Glen and a half hour later turns down a road with a carved wooden sign: a bear pointing with one paw, Lake Winnasaki. And a few minutes later another bear sign, Camp Winnasaki.

With a bullhorn Ms. Thornton booms a greeting. "Welcome, campers!" All the kids crowd over to one side of the bus to see who's talking. "Hel-lo, how-de-do, hi there, and a hocus-pocus." She finds nearly twenty ways to let them know they've arrived while the bus crunches down the gravel road and parks in front of a small log cabin, the kind Abe Lincoln was born in.

Ms. Thornton teaches biology at Cobweb. That's how Mom knows about this camp. She probably conned Ms. Thornton into hiring me without an interview by reminding her that I was dadless. I wonder if Mom told her that I love little kids, a big lie. Ms. Thornton's classroom is full of slimy creatures like garter snakes, which she lets slither up her arm ("and God knows where else," Jenna says). When she dissects a frog, she displays the severed legs on her bare palm. Ms. Thornton always mashes down her voluminous, screaming-red hair with a wide, white headband. The result is not quite a hairdo, more like she went to the hospital and got bandaged. She is covered with freckles, even her legs, which I notice through the bus window because she's wearing baggy plaid shorts.

"Here you go." Mr. DeAngelo swings the kids out, one after another. When Rocco's turn comes, the kid declares, "I'm going to leave the bus backward with my eyes shut." Mr. DeAngelo grabs him anyway. As soon as he lands, Lark shoves Rocco's lunch box right into his chest so he has to hold it, no choice. "Carry your own lunch, dodo bird. And don't talk to me again in public." She is definitely his sister.

Ms. Thornton and several counselors wear white

T-shirts that say CAMP WINNASAKI. All the counselors look to be my age. Well, I look old for my age in my opinion, because of my awesome maturity and possible air of tragedy. Maybe they're older than me. One counselor, a guy with a buzz cut, is doing push-ups. He springs up, performs a few jumping jacks, and shakes his arms to loosen up. I guess you need to be in good shape to handle a bunch of kids under the age of ten.

"Hey, I'm Simon, who are you?" He jogs a circle around me as I trail everyone onto a tennis court that has weeds growing around the edge and cracks in the asphalt, perfect for tripping and falling.

"I'm Frannie." I give him a Mona Lisa smile. The *Mona Lisa* is a famous portrait by Leonardo da Vinci of a woman with long brown hair, wearing a scoop-neck top. Dad showed me a picture of it. The important thing isn't her hair or her clothes—which are nothing to write home about—but her smile. It's mysterious, no teeth showing, lips pressed together but they go up the tiniest bit at the edges.

Dad argued that her smile is mysterious because of her eyes, not her lips. Man, he never shut up about eyes and how they're the key to everything, but I digress, which means to ramble off on a side track giving other people either anxiety or utter boredom. Jenna and I practiced Mona Lisa smiles in front of the mirror. When someone bugged us at school, we would say, Give him (or her) the MLS. With the MLS, it's not clear if you're smiling, being secretive, or, in the case of me with Simon right now, acting superior.

"Frannie," he repeats. "Frannie-bo-banny."

Forget the MLS. A total snub is in order.

"Simon. Simon, raise your hand," calls Ms. Thornton. "Simon teaches canoeing, nature, and sensitivity training."

"Yo, dudes," says Simon.

Sensitivity training. Of course sensitivity—Ms. Thornton teaches at Cobweb. She introduces all the counselors except me, then, in a roll call, divides the campers into groups according to their age.

Everyone should call her Harriet, Ms. Thornton announces. Whichever group stands in the straightest line will get s'mores at the end of the week, she promises.

Lark raises her hand. "Rocco can't eat sugar, he's allergic."

"We'll find something else for you to eat, won't we, Rocco?"

"Me eat flies." Rocco beats his chest.

"That's nice. We'll find you some juicy ones," says Ms. Thornton.

"I rode on a cloud," he adds.

"He did not," Lark calls loudly.

"If I eat sugar, my mom blows a gasket," says a girl wearing a tiara. "It makes me hyper. Except carrot cake. Are we going swimming?"

A bunch of kids start carrying on about how they had carrot cake for their birthdays. I guess it's a popular cake type. Ms. Thornton blares through the bullhorn. "Silence, please." The counselors all put their fingers to their lips to indicate that their campers should obey. Ms. Thornton then disperses the groups to various activities—hiking, canoeing, folk dancing, archery, swimming. I'm the only one left on the tennis court when Harriet notices (it's going to be hard to get used to calling her Harriet) and claps her hands. "Frannie, I forgot you were coming, and we need you desperately. You'll set up in there."

She waves toward a ramshackle barn over near some trees. One side sags, causing the whole struc-

ture to tilt—Dad would love that; maybe he would even have appreciated the tarpaper patches dotting the roof. The side windows must be missing or cracked, because the panes are partially sealed with plastic. Harriet rambles on, "I assume you've got it all worked out. Your mother says you're a complete genius."

At what am I a complete genius? That I would like to know.

Should I admit I'm clueless about the exact nature of the job? It slipped Mom's mind to tell me, probably because she was so busy crying. And it slipped my mind to ask, because I was so busy being agreeable so she'd stop crying.

At that moment Ms. Thornton, aka Harriet, discovers a bird feather. "My goodness, look at that." She snatches it from the ground and holds it out. "Can you make use of this in your arts and crafts program?"

So I am the arts and crafts counselor.

A revolting discovery. I don't know anything about arts and crafts. I draw. D-R-A-W. Art is serious. Arts and crafts—that's making-potholder time. Trust Mom not to know the difference.

I consider screaming. Can I simply open my mouth in the middle of Camp Winnasaki and howl? For the next eight weeks I'm expected to ride here every day in a bus full of shrieking brats and teach them arts and crafts, something about which I know nothing, when I should be home doing the puzzle.

I leave Harriet Thornton and walk to the barn.

"I'll send over your first victims in an hour." She honks a laugh. Her laugh is famous at Cobweb for resembling the call of an elephant.

The barn door refuses to budge. Shoulder first, I throw my weight against it, and it creaks open a few inches, revealing a glimpse of the impediment: a gigantic bale of hay. I squeeze in and then, using my nonexistent muscles, inch the bale away from the door.

It's nice inside. How unexpected. Sunlight seeps in between loose shingles, and the whole effect is mellow yellow. Straw on the floor, musty smell, old things. To me, comfort food. There's a large metal windmilly thing—maybe part of a thresher. Although I'm not sure what a thresher is, for some reason that word comes to mind. Dad would have popped his cork over its lovely shape of interlocking circles. He'd have leaped around, viewed it from every angle. The only eyesore—a metal table, quite long, leaning against the wall with a few stacks of folding chairs—must be for my nonexistent arts-and-crafts program. I look around for shelves or a cabinet. None. No supplies as far as I can tell. What is the Honker thinking?

The table, all rusted, makes skin-shivering squeaks as I unfold the legs. Several times it crashes over. That's my klutzy fault. I set up the chairs around it—now I'm wiped from the most exertion I've had in months. I collapse in a chair and stare half-wittedly at the floor, an activity I highly recommend for brain dulling. Soon the floor begins to seem inviting, and the next thing I know—the urge is too compelling—I lie down on it.

Straw prickles my neck, the hard wood chafes my shoulder blades. Gazing up, I notice spiderwebs in the crossbeams, a jagged lightning bolt of a crack in the ceiling, a certain musical quality to the shifting light patterns. I swear there is melody in light. What I mean is, you can think of the wind and the sun and the clouds, even time—all the elements that combine to affect color and the nature of light—as an orchestra playing different tunes in different combinations every second of the day. Dum, de, dum, dum.

I almost cease to exist lying there.

The ground vibrates. How bizarre, although interesting. Then I realize why. Small feet thundering in. Seven-year-olds peer down at me, and looming over, Harriet the Honker. Her forehead crinkles, eyes narrow, probably wondering what sort of weirdo she has on her hands.

"I'm getting horizontal," I offer by way of explanation. Her forehead furrows until there's a crease you could dive into. I am freaking the lady out.

I stand and brush off the straw. Harriet picks a few bits out of my hair.

"What's horizontal?" asks a boy, scratching his sides.

"Are you itchy?"

"I have twelve mosquito bites." He lifts his T-shirt. "One, two, three . . ." He counts nine red spots on his stomach, two on his arm, and one on his ankle.

"What's your name?"

"Brandon."

"Well, Brandon with the twelve bites, getting horizontal is an official art term. It means lying down."

"I'm Pearl. Who are you?" says the girl in the tiara.

"Frannie."

Rocco is using the thresher-sculpture as a jungle gym.

"Please get down from there, Rocco," I say.

"No." He leaps, grabbing at a higher bar.

"Rocco!" I might have shrieked, I'm not sure. I grab his legs and hug them to my chest. "Let go, right now." He flops over my shoulder, and I deposit him back on the ground. He waves me to come close.

"What?" I ask.

He cups his hands around his mouth. "The moon is a marble."

"Who told you that?"

"Me. I can cut the sky in two."

"Oh, well, okay. Stay down here, do you understand? Stay off that, whatever it is."

"Have fun," says the Honker, suddenly satisfied, and she splits.

I chase her. "Ms. Thornton. Harriet."

She stops.

"I can't do this, I don't want to do this. This was my mom's idea."

"Aw, Frannie." She puts her arms around me. "Hug time." My face smashes into her shoulder. She pats my back as if prompting a burp.

This is so embarrassing. So embarrassing to be someone anyone can make cry. I mean, one hug from Harriet Honker Thornton is all it takes. How humiliating. To avoid a flash flood, I have to freeze my face, make it rock solid, a difficult thing to accomplish. Fortunately she releases me.

I focus on her freckles. "But what am I supposed to do?"

"I have no idea. Do whatever you want." She

blows a piercing blast on her whistle. "Hey there, Jesse, wait up." She signals another counselor and strides off.

"Excuse me."

I turn.

She must have been here all along but I hadn't noticed. An extremely neat person: an ENP. Her Camp Winnasaki T-shirt is tucked into pressed khaki shorts. As for my obsession, hair. Hers (in a ponytail) behaves: Not one strand escapes from the velvet scrunchee. She's at least eighteen years old— I can tell from her poise. I don't know anyone my age who is truly confident. Not even Sukie Jameson, in spite of her curves and straight-A average. When Sukie gave an oral report on the African-American Civil War Brigade, her voice trembled. The reason I know the ENP has poise to burn is that she asks a question as if it wasn't one. She says, "I'll come back later, do you mind?" But she implies, "I'll come back later, tough noogies if you mind."

The ENP is gorgeous, something everyone in

a random survey would agree on. Golden-brown hair, flawless coppery skin, a perfectly proportioned straight-and-narrow nose, and royal-blue eyes, small but startling. Excuse me while I experience envy.

"You don't have to stay," I tell the ENP unnecessarily as we cross paths, me returning to the little monsters, she on the exit route.

"'Bye, Eagles," she calls.

"'Bye," they all shout back.

"Okay, everyone—horizontal." I snap my fingers.

"Horizontal," the Barbie girls instruct their dolls, placing them on the floor, as all the Eagles lie down and start complaining about how prickly it is, except for one girl who remains standing. My mom stuck rubber daisies on the bottom of the shower so I wouldn't slip, and the shower floor looks exactly like the fabric on this girl's pants.

"What's the matter?" I ask Daisy Pants.

"I'll get dirty."

"You're supposed to get dirty. All great artists get dirty." I don't know this for a fact, but can you imagine a great artist, about to paint a masterpiece, getting vexed and anxious, Uh-oh, I hope paint doesn't drip on me?

"What's your name?"

"Hazel."

"It smells in here. It smells like poop," says Rocco.

"It doesn't smell like poop. What you smell is a good smell, it's nature. You can watch," I tell Hazel, who is still standing and now holding her nose. "Okay, everyone, I want absolute silence, because what we are going to do is the most important thing in the world."

To my amazement, they all shut up.

"To be an artist, you have to use your eyes. Look up. What do you see?"

"Poop," shouts Rocco.

"If your eyes are closed, you can't see," Hazel points out.

"Keep your eyes open."

Rocco rolls around, coating himself with straw.

"Poop, poop, poop." He rolls into the wall. He rolls into another camper, who kicks him. Rocco kicks him back, and then there's a pile-up of campers pummeling, and the Barbie twins bawl that someone kicked their dolls, and Pearl shrieks that her tiara got bent. I scream at the top of my lungs, "Stop."

And everyone does, except Pearl.

Forget art. Forget seeing. Forget it all.

The kids, all jumbled on the ground, begin to disentangle.

"I have an idea," I say. "Do you know what poison is?"

14

Poison is a riveting subject. I hold them spellbound. We devise a project. They leave, and the eight-to-tens arrive. Poison is riveting to them, too. Harriet said I should do what I want, and that's exactly what I'm doing. They get their instructions. They know what they have to find at home and bring to camp tomorrow. Before I leave, I give Harriet a list of supplies: glue, cardboard, masking tape, and scissors. Enough scissors for everyone. And markers.

The campers don't clown around as much on the

way home. Several fall asleep, and the only incident is that, when I look down, Rocco's head is next to my shoes. He's chewing my laces.

"I'm a dog," he says when I haul him out.

The trip feels endless. I'm dying to get back to the puzzle. From now on, when I'm on the bus, I'm going to plug in my iPod. It will make the time pass faster and keep the kids from bugging me. Besides, I'm happier when I'm somewhere else, somewhere not a place, more a space.

The campers yell, "'Bye, Frannie," when I get off, and some pound the windows. I guess it's easy to be popular when you don't want to be.

I should give my mom the silent treatment for forcing me into this awful job, although . . . bad idea. Rule: If you want to get your mother's attention, act mad.

I will act happy.

Not too happy. That will confuse her. Just happy enough so that she leaves me in peace.

After checking my room to reassure myself that

the puzzle is still there, I hang out with Mom. She chops garlic while Mel gets out glasses and a bottle of wine. There's a TV in the kitchen, and on the screen a man and a woman ice-skate on a pond in a wooded glen. The woman does some twirls.

"Perfume," says my mom.

"Deodorant," says Mel.

They love to guess what the commercials are advertising. They seem intentionally to guess wrong because it makes them laugh. In this one, after the man and woman skate awhile, the ice turns to ground, so now they're walking, the ground grows long grass, and in the middle of the field is an SUV. Mom and Mel find this wildly funny.

"How did it go today?" she asks.

Mel, uncorking the wine, pauses for my response.

"Vile. Harriet Thornton is a lunatic."

Lunatic is one of my very favorite words. *Eyeballs* is another. I like *lunatic* because of the sound. It's fun to pronounce. Also, *luna* means moon in some other language, Greek or Latin. So the word *lunatic* suggests that the moon has driven you crazy. What a shivery notion. As for *eyeballs* . . . that word's kind of comical. *Eyeballs*. Try to work it into normal conversation and see if you don't agree.

"Do you want me to set the table?" I ask.

"Yes, thank you. Are there any counselors you might be friends with?"

I think about Simon and the ENP. "No, they're all awful. What's for dinner?"

"Pasta and spinach salad. What kind of arts-and-crafts projects will you be doing?"

I ignore the question. "Harriet stuck me in a barn so rickety, it will probably collapse and kill me." Oops, I didn't mean to say that, it slipped out. I meant to keep the conversation innocuous. Fortunately, she doesn't react because Mel breaks off the cork, leaving half of it stuck in the bottle. His lame move provokes a mini fit—they have to shove the cork down and strain the wine to extract cork bits. The wine is saved, and so am I. Tra la. I can retreat to my bedroom and work the puzzle uninterrupted until dinner and begin again immediately after.

I'm assembling the largest of those ancient Irish houses around the cove. From my beautiful box I cull the reds: reddish brown for the roof tiles and reddish pink for the walls. Here are some red with green spots. The shutters are green. I isolate those, too. What's this? A red piece with a splash of yellow? I study the photo. I can't locate red and yellow together, not on this building or any other. I drop that piece back into the box bottom, along with the rest of the unsorted.

Lying on my tummy, I work steadily for hours. The night is windy and the brush of branches against my window keeps me company. Each time I make a match, I see something unexpected. The edge of the red house, flat in the photo, acquires dimension. Maybe it isn't flush against the lilac one next door. I imagine someone walking around the side, disappearing down an alley so ancient and narrow that buildings on opposite sides can almost kiss.

My eyes ache. I need a break.

I prop myself up on my elbows, planting one elbow in the box right on top of the puzzle pieces. I close my eyes, dizzy for a moment. When I lift my arm, ready to resume, a puzzle piece sticks to it—the same red piece with the splash of yellow that I tossed back earlier. I try it, and it clicks into place on the red house. I find myself looking at a window. A window with a yellow light inside.

I check the photo again. No window with a light. This detail must be too small to show up in the small snapshot. Is this really a window? I lean close to the puzzle. The yellow brightens to an intense pinpoint glow. My eyes snap closed; I jerk back, try to focus again, and start blinking. A light is shining straight into my eyes. I hold up my hand, blocking the glare, and peek between my fingers. I'm looking at a small round dented brass lamp. It has a little brass cap perched on top of a glowing yellow bulb. That lamp isn't mine. Neither is the tall, skinny bureau it sits on. I've never seen them before.

I turn away. I'm no longer on the floor. No longer in my room. That's not my door. A sign hangs from the knob. Not in English. Oh, yes, there is an English sentence. GUESTS MUST LEAVE BY NOON. This instruction appears to be in four languages. Spanish, too, I recognize that. Two others, unfamiliar. GUESTS MUST LEAVE BY NOON. My brain operates at tortoise speed. Am I a guest? Is that an instruction for me? The floor feels rough. I recognize my own bare feet but not the itchy coarse carpet. I recognize my dad's shirt and my jeans, the clothes I'm wearing. I spin around. There's a bed—a double bed covered with a thin gray blanket that has a cigarette burn and two pillows flat as planks. What a small, shabby place this is. The bed and bureau almost eat the room. A suitcase juts from under the bed, the cardboard suitcase I saw in Dad's studio. Next to that are two backpacks, both open, with clothes falling out.

I hear rain. Only let me tell you, I hear it for a

while before I hear it. I mean, there's this pitter-patter happening, but it doesn't penetrate, and then, oh, wow, rain. Curtains block the only window. I push them to the side.

White. I see nothing but white. I unlatch the old brass window lock, the kind Dad might scavenge from a dump and make a speech about: They don't make locks like this anymore, feel the weight, blah, blah, blah. When I push it, the window slides open but barely, because the rusty metal hardware jams.

I squeeze my hand through the narrow opening and my hand evaporates. I yank my hand back inside. It's intact, all five fingers. Did that actually happen? I slip my hand back out, and again the fog swallows it: My arm ends at my wrist. This fog is as thick as frosting.

I snake my hand back inside, getting scratched in the process. This decrepit wooden window frame badly needs sanding.

Anyway, there's no rain.

Of course, no rain. Pitter-patter but no rain.

I walk toward another door, a door I thought led to a closet.

Once I nail it—not rain but shower—that pitter-patter fills my head to the brim. The steady flow from a showerhead. Not a closet, a bathroom. "Hello," I say.

No answer.

I call loudly, "Hello."

"Laura?"

My dad. It's my dad. I want to shout, "Not Mom, me. It's me, Dad," but maybe I faint. Maybe my legs crumple, because I'm looking at them and they're lying limply, and grass appears to be growing around them, only it's not grass. It's the fuzzy green rug on the floor of my room.

"Showers expected later today will move through the region quickly. . . ."

My clock radio. Daylight.

15

It's taking all my energy not to fall into the Rice Krispies.

I droop over the table, my chin hovers above the bowl. I barely have the strength to lift the spoon. A strange and powerful dream can do that, wear you out and frazzle you. Sleeping on the floor, and for only two hours, can't help either. Mel, filling his thermos, glances up. "Are you all right?"

"I'm fine." I put my tonsils on display, yawning widely.

The route of least exertion is to drink the Rice

Krispies, so I cup the bowl in my hands, lift it, and slurp, making dreadful sucking sounds, grossing Mel out. Confession: Irritating Mel gives me energy; it's like a little protein boost.

As soon as I get on the bus, an assault: The kids clamor to show me what they brought for the arts-and-crafts project. Seat backs rattle. Their shrieks are deafening, the war whoops of advancing troops. My poor woozy head. "Later, later, wait until camp, I need to meditate." I drop into my seat.

Brandon clonks me from behind. "What's meditate?"

"Meditate means listen to music." I plug in my iPod and zone out.

I avoid the Honker and everyone else. At the morning get-together I loiter in the background, keeping my head down. When I trek to the barn, however, Simon brays, "Frannie. Frannie-Bananie."

Foolishly, kind of knee-jerk without thinking, I look over, and he shouts, "Marry me. Marry me and be my canoe."

Tucking my head down, I speed on. I hate my mother. How could she force me to work in a place where a guy asks me to be his canoe? What *is* that? That is so strange, there is probably no name for it. Eyes on the grass, don't look up. I almost collide with the barn, also Mom's fault.

Inside I find my supplies lumped on the table. Oh, good, a nice boring task. Something mindless. I arrange neat piles: scissors, glue, cardboard, tape. The Honker has also provided a stack of empty boxes for storage. I label them and put the markers away. I'm hoping to squeeze in some lie-on-the-floor time, but the Eagles arrive.

After toting their backpacks and, in Hazel's case, towing in a round pink patent-leather suitcase on wheels, they unpack their contributions to our art project, a gigantic poison collage. Dad and I made collages all the time when I was younger. Once, when I glued a doll's arm in the middle of a collage of Archie and Veronica comics, Dad declared that my "choice" was brilliant. I swear, I could have thrown paint at the wall, drawn blind-folded, or dropped ketchup on a drawing by accident because I was eating a hamburger while I worked, and Dad would have hailed it as a choice. "The artist never does anything by accident," he insisted. He made everything I did seem grand.

The Eagles have collected a heap of household cleaners. Several campers have brought things I mentioned: toothpaste, dishwashing detergent, detergent for clothes. Rocco empties his pockets of several double-A batteries. I read the label. "'Batteries may explode, causing burn injury.' Excellent. Thank you, Rocco."

I examine other stuff. A box of mothballs. "May be fatal if inhaled." I have to explain what *fatal* means, and one of the Barbie twins doesn't under-stand the word *inhale*. Hazel unzips her suitcase and, after showing me her new swimsuit, presents me with a bottle of Listerine. In a loud voice, she reads, "'If more than used for rinsing is acciden-tally swallowed, get medical help or contact a

Poison Control Center right away.'"

"A major discovery," I declare, while confiscating another double-A battery that Rocco has stuck in his ear. "Hazel, I congratulate you. Take a bow. This is mouthwash, a wash for your mouth, and yet, if gulped, dangerous. Does everyone get how cuckoo that is? One false move, like let's say you were gargling and saw a mouse . . ."

They all erupt with various other ways they might be shocked into taking huge gulps of Listerine, including spotting a ghost or a zombie. "If you were watching a PG-13 movie, that could cause it," says Hazel.

"If your brother put a bug down your shirt," adds Isabel, a bouncy girl cursed with a gigantic head of wiry curls. Her hair is light pinky brown, the color of a dry hippopotamus, and her curls are like a cloud, light and airy. You see them and see through them at the same time, a bit bizarre.

Isabel has no idea that her hair is unfortunate. I can tell because she's in perpetual happy motion, jumping, twirling. When she talks, she cocks her head and leans right into my face, then jumps away the minute she's done. Everything I say makes her clap with excitement. When she's eleven, someone like Sukie will break the news that her hair is the color of a dry hippopotamus, and depression will ensue.

One of the Barbie twins tugs my sleeve. "What happened to your hand?"

"Can I sit on your lap?" asks the other.

Both these questions are completely off the subject, and besides I am not even sitting down, but Barbie Two doesn't wait for an answer. She raises her arms. I lift her and sit. She slumps against me, with her doll tight against her chest. At that moment it occurs to me that I can run the project seated. Wouldn't that take less energy? Perhaps I'll never have to get up—I can direct the mob from the chair for the whole summer. So, speaking over Barbie Two's head, I divide them into two groups: One group will put together the small pieces of cardboard to make one giant board to glue the collage on—and knowing a bossy type when I see one, I put Hazel in charge of that task. The other group does the cutting: warning labels, brand names, any images on the boxes they want to include in the collage. Rocco does neither. He jabbers about a dead rat under the garage, staggers around, and falls to show me how the rat, poisoned by Lark, died. He loves the staggering and dying part. He keeps doing it over and over and then asks if I want to see the rat. His dad dropped a brick and smashed it flat.

"I thought Lark poisoned it."

He ignores that remark. "Do you want to see it? It's under my pillow."

There's no way this rat is under his pillow. "I'd love to."

Barbie One tugs me again. "Did you cut it?"

"Cut what?"

"Your hand. Did a cat scratch it? My cat scratched me."

"I didn't cut my hand." I hold it out to show her.

She turns my hand over so the palm faces down.

The back is pink and puffy. I look closely. A splinter.

16

JENNA'S MOM throws out her arms. What choice do I have? "Guess who's here," she shouts after squeezing me. "Frannie. It's Frannie."

Jenna's face appears upstairs, over the banister. Alice, their housekeeper, rushes out of the kitchen. Another hug. I dread them. I should hang a NO HUGS sign around my neck. "Mambo, look who's here." Jenna's mom nudges the dog, who's napping. Mambo flaps his tail once as if he's swatting a fly.

I take the stairs two at a time, drag Jenna into her room, and shut the door. "I have to talk to you."

"I can't believe you're here," Jenna says, "because I was just thinking that I have to talk to *you*. The most unbelievable thing has happened."

"Same here."

"Really?"

"Really."

In case you're wondering why we're acting as if I haven't ignored her for three whole months, you know what? It didn't matter.

"What happened, Frannie?"

I can't quite come out with it. Ever since Barbie One pointed out the splinter, I've been obsessed, *Get to Jenna, you've got to get to Jenna,* but now here I am and she's waiting. . . . "You first," I say.

Jenna assumes first position. In ballet, it's a way of standing so your heels are together and your toes point out. That's what she does when she's excited. Most kids jump up and down. Jenna snaps into first position, her back straight as a ruler, long neck extended. She goes still. She practically quivers with stillness. When Dad and I were at the beach on

Cape Cod, we saw, at the water's edge, a graceful little bird with long legs as skinny as string. "A sandpiper," Dad said. Perhaps if you were close, you could see its feathers ruffle, but through the binoculars from our perch at the top of a dune, the little bird looking out to sea appeared unmoving, elegant, taut with expectation. "That bird reminds me of Jenna," said Dad, and I knew exactly what he meant.

"James is a chef." Jenna's voice goes all hush-hush when she's in first position, as if everything she says is so earth-shattering it can't be spoken in a normal tone.

"A chef? In a restaurant?"

"No, not in a restaurant, at home."

"You mean he cooks? He's a cook?"

"Oh, Frannie, don't do that."

I don't ask because I know. "Sorry."

"He means a lot to me."

"Okay, so Dr. Dental Floss is a chef."

"Frannie!"

"Sorry. Go on. I'm sorry, Jenna."

"His parents were out and he made me spaghetti with sausage and cabbage, which sounds disgusting but it is so excellent. You should see him. He chops like he's on *Iron Chef*. He loves *Iron Chef*."

"Is that what you wanted to tell me?"

"Almost. He asked me to cut the price tag off his apron. He gave me poultry shears to do it."

"What are poultry shears?"

"Big scissors. He has every piece of kitchen equipment you could ever need. Three whisks, even a tiny one like for a doll. He uses it for salad dressing."

I try to imagine Waldo loping around the kitchen, juggling pots and pans, wearing oven mitts. I like the idea of him in oven mitts.

"Are you listening?"

Jenna's sensitive to when my brain spins into orbit. "I'm listening, go on."

"The tag was in front—it's this white chef's apron with a bib—and I could smell him and he smelled of onions because he'd just been chopping them, and he said, 'Taste this.' He stuck out his tongue and we licked tongues."

"So you and James are together?"

Jenna props her leg on the dresser and arches her body over it. She's unpredictable. Just when you think she's going to sigh and moan, she decides to give her muscles a stretch. "Remember the Satin Ultra lip gloss we got? It comes right off."

"You mean from kissing."

"From kissing," she says, proud to have that knowledge. "From anything. It doesn't last at all, it's kind of a rip-off, but the good thing is that it keeps your lips moist. What a surprise. What an awesome incredible surprise."

"Most lip gloss comes off pretty easily."

"Not the lip gloss. James. When we licked, and then later when he sprinkled basil on the pasta and lit candles, I kept thinking, 'Is this my life? I can't believe this is my life.' Remember when we thought we'd never get breasts, and then we did? And then I thought I'll never have truly romantic experiences, and now I'm having them. Isn't this unbelievable? What happened to you?"

I can't answer right away because she's reminded me of all the things we fantasized at a million sleepovers. Things are happening to her that she wished for, and the thing that happened to me is at the very top of my not-wished-for list, or would be if I'd ever made one. Once Jenna and I moped for weeks because Sukie claimed she was having wild sex with a football player at Hudson High while we were still practicing puckers in the mirror. Will I ever get bummed out about something silly again, or am I permanently bummed out about something colossal? I want to have no perspective about what matters and what doesn't. I want to lose my marbles over basil. Instead I'm dying to point out how dumb it all is, big deal, he sprinkles basil. So what, he's got an itty-bitty whisk. I want her to feel awful. I want everyone to feel awful, because I do. It's wretched but true.

I can stick Jenna with a giant dose of perspective.

Or I can tell her this bizarre thing.

Scold or tell. Insult or confide.

Tell, tell, tell.

I flop on the bed. Jenna climbs on too, only she sits up cross-legged while I lie like a limp trout. After all, I'm fairly wiped out—not sleeping, the job, massive agitation from the latest turn of events. I begin at the beginning, finding Dad's present. It's exciting to tell her and a total relief. I linger over details: the exquisitely carved box, the intricate Celtic knots contrasting with the simple stark lettering of FRANCES ANNE 1000. I confess that I embroider, inventing some thumping heartbeats and sweaty palms before I eased off the top. I also exaggerate the danger of being discovered, my mom's nosiness—claiming I barely sneaked the box by her while she endured the pennywhistle music. Jenna makes a hideous face as she always does at even a mention of that crazy bird music.

"How strange is it that Dad finished my present early? That is—was . . ." I stop. "How unlike him."

"Imagine carving a thousand-piece puzzle by hand."

Just like that, Jenna solves the mystery of the 1000. One thousand means one thousand pieces. To her it's obvious, and I knew she'd nailed it. The explanation fits like a puzzle piece when it's the right match.

"One thousand." Jenna shakes her head. "How long did it take him? Do you think your dad spent over a year? Maybe two? Wow."

My eyes water up; man the floodgates. That is the tenderest notion—Dad toiling away for maybe two years to make me a birthday present. I tell Jenna about the photo, how the puzzle must be a scene from a town in Ireland where my grandparents were born. "Oh, oh, oh, I almost forgot. I took the photo to the Xerox place to make an enlargement and it didn't work. The colors ran, although that's scientifically impossible; still the photo looked all streaked and blurry, as if they had. The photo couldn't be copied."

"You're giving me goose bumps, Frannie. Feel my arm." Sure enough, she has prickles up and down it. "James has a whole notebook filled with recipes he Xeroxed."

"What does that have to do with anything?"

"It doesn't. Sorry."

I'm not sure I want to confide in Jenna after all. "Are you planning to tell James all about this?"

"No."

"Do you swear?"

"I swear."

"No matter what he does with his tongue?"

That makes us both laugh. "Say it. Say, 'I swear, no matter what he does with his tongue or if he says my eyes are beautiful black beans and my breath smells of eggplant.'"

Jenna has a fit of giggles, even snorts a few times, before she can swear. Then I confide the strangest part: the dream. I show her my hand. "If

I have a splinter, then maybe it wasn't a dream. Maybe I was there."

It's spookily silent at that instant. Outside, no whoosh of cars down the block or shudder of leaves in the wind. Jenna touches my splinter lightly with her finger. We both gaze at the sliver of wood, the only evidence of my preposterous claim.

"Tell me about the dream again," Jenna says finally.

I run through it once more. The room with the cardboard suitcase under the bed, the sign on the door. "It must be a hotel room, right?" Seeing nothing out the window but white.

"Fog?" asks Jenna.

"I guess. When I put my hand out the window, it was like my hand evaporated. I couldn't see it. I could sense it, I knew it was there, but it was invisible."

"Invisible," Jenna echoes.

"If it was fog, it was the world's thickest. Also, you know what, now that I'm thinking about it—"

"What?"

"Fog is wet, isn't it?"

"Wet?"

"You can kind of feel fog. It's moist and cool, but this white stuff, it didn't feel like that."

"What did it feel like?"

"I guess not really anything. Anyway, when I pulled my hand back inside, I scraped it on the window frame. I felt it, Jenna. I remember noticing that the wood on the frame was shredding."

Jenna taps her teeth with her thumbnail, a thing she does when she's thinking.

"Impossible, right? I'm crazy. Demented." I roll off the bed.

She nods.

"I can't have fallen into a jigsaw puzzle. It's only a dream, one of those exceptionally real ones where you wake up and are completely shocked to find that you were, in fact, actually dreaming." I open the desk drawer where Jenna sometimes stashes protein bars. There's nothing but a half-shriveled carrot. "This is gross."

Jenna drops it into the wastebasket. "White out the window, no world at all—that's a dream thing for sure. Is there someplace else you could have gotten a splinter?"

I have to admit it. "I could have gotten it at Camp Winnasaki, in the barn."

I hold out my hand, and we both study it as if it were a science exhibit. Is there a clue in the little splinter and the pink irritated skin around it? "Shouldn't we remove it?" Jenna asks.

"It's my only proof."

· 163 ·

"You might get an infection."

"I'll risk it."

"Let's go."

"Where?"

"Frannie, you've got to show me the puzzle."

17

Jenna gets the same enthusiastic greeting at my place that I got at hers. My mom screeches and practically does backflips. Mel is summoned. They are so happy and relieved to see Jenna that it bugs me. Like this is proof that I'm over Dad's death or something. A good side effect: Mom is exceptionally pliant, letting us eat dinner privately in my room, delivering the chicken and rice on paper plates with plastic knives and forks for both of us. I'm sure Jenna thinks, given the paper and plastic, that Mom is doing an indoor-picnic thing, when she's actually doing a don't-let-Jenna-know-Frannie-is-crazy thing.

"Mom, what town did Dad's mom and dad come from?"

"Albany."

"No, I mean in Ireland. Before they came here."

"Oh. I'm not sure. Blarney, Blaney, Blantry. Something with a *B*. Why? Did you find something in his stuff?"

"What would I find?"

"I don't know. Why did you ask?"

"There's this guy at camp, Simon, who's always talking about Ireland."

"Who's Simon?" asks my mom.

"No one."

I have no idea why I blame Ireland on Simon. I don't even know why I brought him up. "Great chicken, Mom."

"Thank you."

As soon as she leaves, I explain all about Simon, how he's revolting and irrelevant, and then I slide the treasures out from under the bed.

Jenna views the carved box from every angle, caresses the wood, admires the chiseling of my name. *"Frances Anne,"* she whispers. "So elegant. Your dad was amazing."

Jenna's not a rusher. She takes her time. That's probably why she's good at applying eye makeup. Bizarre, isn't it? Being awfully skilled and patient at drawing lines around the eyes wouldn't seem to indicate that a person would also be a great appreciator, but nevertheless, at least with Jenna, those two great gifts go together. When I lift the top off the box, she combs through the puzzle pieces, oohing and aahing over the intricate cutting and painting.

"You know what this is, Frannie?" she says.

"What?"

"An act of love."

An act of love. Fact, not opinion. My chest tightens. I have to flop onto the floor, on my back, and go into ceiling mode. You know how hair dryers have settings—high, low, and off? Well, I'm beginning to think that I have settings—awake, sleep, and ceiling. Jenna is too busy comparing the snapshot to the work I've completed on the puzzle to notice that I'm zoning out.

"Is this the window? The upstairs one?" she asks.

"Yes," I agree without actually checking to see what's she's referring to. Lying here is calming, although . . . while I'm familiar with some wrinkles in my bedroom ceiling, the result of multiple repaintings before we even moved in, now I detect spidery cracks. "A friend of Mom's, this woman Rachel, was going to the bathroom when the ceiling fell on her."

Apparently Jenna is preoccupied with the puzzle, because she responds, "Show me exactly what happened."

"I don't really remember. I was looking at the puzzle and then I was in it."

She waves the snapshot over my face. "Try it again."

I lean close to the puzzle, close enough to lick it. I stay there, immobile.

"Stare."

"I am."

"Hard. Until your head gets dizzy. Remember how we used to stand in front of the mirror until our eyes crossed and our faces got fuzzy? Try that."

I try it. It feels stupid. This whole idea is stupid. I fell asleep while I was working a jigsaw puzzle and had a dream. That's all.

Jenna knows it's stupid too. Neither of us needs to say it.

I slide the puzzle back under the bed.

"How very cool." Jenna pulls the board out and shoves it back—out and in, out and in. "Did you make this?"

"I ripped the back off mom's ugly old bookcase and stripped the casters off a chair."

"James is pretty handy too," says Jenna.

I let her carry on about a card he made for her. He cut out a magazine picture of a chef wearing a professional outfit complete with tall hat and glued a photo of his face over the chef's face. Then he found a picture of a roast chicken and pasted on Jenna's photo, the one from the yearbook, so it looked like the chicken had her head. He glued chef and chicken to a construction-paper heart, signed it "James à la mode," and tucked it in her biology book, along with a sprig of rosemary. It was pretty dumb (an understatement), and made no logical sense (*à la mode* means with ice cream, so what does that have to do with a chicken and a sprig of rosemary?), but Jenna lights up when she describes it. She couldn't look happier if she won the lottery or heard that she never has to go to gym again. Her idiotic card has nothing to do with my puzzle board. How can a person compare a scissor-and-glue job to carpentry? But hey, Jenna is my very best friend, the best and the greatest. It's sweet that she can't stop grinning when she talks about James. Love is blind. I don't think I realized the utter truth of that until I heard Jenna rhapsodize about having her head on a chicken.

18

A partial list of contributions to the poison collage.

    dishwashing detergent

    toothpaste

    mouthwash

    hair spray

    one red apple

    mothballs

    AA batteries

    nail polish remover

Gregor, a boy in the older group who contributes the apple, has a wishing face—hopeful, longing, sweet. Every time I look at him, I wonder what he wants to hear. "It began with the apple," he says.

"Are you referring to Eve, in the Bible?"

"No. Snow White."

"Mirror, mirror on the wall, who is the fairest of us all?" I cackle, and they all laugh except Lark, who points out that we can't put the apple in the collage because it will rot.

"Rotting is good," I tell her. "Poisons pollute the world; the apple will pollute the collage. We'll be making a statement. Let's have one bite out of the apple." I hand it to Gregor.

He turns it few times, and then, satisfied with the location, crunches. He doesn't chew and swallow but removes the bite whole from his mouth. "Use the bite, too," he says.

"What a great idea. You have the makings of a true artist." I don't know why I'm moved to proclaim that, but he beams a whole mouthful of braces.

Lark contributes the hair spray and a speech she's composed on the computer. The title is "Aerosol." "In conclusion," she writes, "aerosol is known to contain chlorofluorocarbons that break down the ozone and cause global warming. The ice caps will melt and we will all drown."

The warnings on the nail polish remover are numerous. Naturally, *Don't swallow.* That's the route to disaster with all these products. In this case I suppose swallowing can occur if you get polish remover confused with cough medicine. Let's say you forget to turn the light on in the bathroom in the middle of the night, which is when my coughing fits usually take place. (Middle of the night is an especially hazardous time. Once, during a sleepover, I opened Jenna's medicine cabinet and took out a tube of diaper rash ointment meant for her baby brother, squeezed it on my toothbrush, and began brushing.) If that happens—if, in some mixed-up moment, you swallow polish remover—*call Poison Control and drink a lot of water.* Also, according to the label, you might go up in flames if you smoke and remove polish at the same time.

We're sitting around the table working on the collage while Celeste, the girl who brought in the polish remover, regales us with these many warnings. She finishes with "harmful to synthetic fabrics, wood finishes, and plastic."

By now I have the campers trained. They whoop with disbelief. "Are your nails tougher than wood?" I scream like a cheerleader. "No," they shout. "Does this make sense?" Again they shout, "No."

Harriet brings her freckles around regularly, although usually she simply stands in the barn door. "Love to see you all as busy as bees," she calls. Today she enters and circles the table while we consider how to include Lark's essay on aerosol (whether or not to cut it up and highlight words like *ozone*). Harriet has to be impressed. The heavy paper is all patched into one gigantic sheet and one quarter patterned with an artful arrangement of labels and warnings, complete with arrows, exclamation points, and dead flowers (Hazel's idea), and a drawing of a skull and crossbones. I consider how my dad would present the project to Harriet. "This work is a collision of art and science," I say.

"What's wrong with your hand?" she asks.

"Oh, this. Just a scrape." I wave off her concerns about the large Band-Aid across the knuckles that protects the splinter so it won't dislodge by accident.

"I've had several calls," she says, "from parents."

I'm not surprised. They send their kids to this goofy camp and never expect them to get a real education. Not only are they becoming artists, but they're being turned from mindless automatons into kids who question Listerine. The parents must be ecstatic. Perhaps Harriet will suggest an art show, framing the work or even getting it hung in the Hudson Glen city hall.

After Harriet has surveyed our work from every angle, she stops behind me. I feel her breath on my neck, a bit creepy, before she whispers in my ear, "When Brandon's dad was replacing a flashlight battery, Brandon told him, 'You could die from that.'"

I swing around. "He really gets it."

"So his father had a little chat with him, and Brandon told him about your art project."

"Didn't he already know? I mean, they've all brought in contributions."

"Well, they knew, but . . ." Harriet takes my arm, elevates me out of my chair, and steers me outside as she calls over her shoulder to the kids, "We'll be right back."

"I suppose it's my fault," she remarks as soon as we're outdoors.

"Fault?"

"I told you to do whatever you wanted. I should have paid more attention when your mother said . . ." She pauses.

"What did my mom say?"

She presses her lips together while she considers what to reply. "Your mom said that you were a little upset. About your dad. Natural, of course. Beatrice is having nightmares."

For a second I can't place Beatrice, but then I remember, of course, Barbie One. "Nightmares about what?"

"What do you think?"

"I don't know."

Harriet chatters on. "Hazel's mother called too. She took Hazel with her to the beauty salon, and Hazel told everyone they would die from hair spray. Hazel tried to hold her breath the whole time she was there, although, of course, she failed. Isabel won't use anything that's been washed in the dishwasher."

"Neither will I."

"Oh, Frannie." She throws her arms around me. "That is sad."

I push her away. Apparently Harriet has the sensitivity of an army tank, because she doesn't back off. She rearranges my hair, tucking it behind my ears while she gives me a super tragic look. "Rocco's dad is the president of this camp."

"This camp has a president?"

"It's nonprofit and he runs it. So he's like a president. He's very important. Rocco has been going around the house saying, 'This kills, that kills.' Finally his father asked, 'What in the world are you talking about?' and Lark filled him in. I don't like to get calls from Rocco's dad, Frannie. This has to stop."

"What has to stop?"

She swoops back into the barn. "All right, everybody." She claps her hands. "Stop what you're doing—we're going to have a nature hike. It's a beautiful day, no arts and crafts." She pulls kids out of their chairs. "Leave those glue dispensers right where they are. Simon's waiting for you."

As she herds them out, she plots, confiding as if we're in cahoots. "We'll think of some way to get their minds off all this, and we'll have to throw it away."

"It?"

"This project of yours."

I stop in my tracks. What? She wants to get rid of it? What nerve. "Wait." I catch up and grab her arm. "You can't do that."

"I know, it will be a little tricky." Again, that conspiratorial tone: "We'll have to tell the kids that some parents are upset."

"Upset? By art! Art is *supposed* to shock you."

Harriet actually laughs. What's funny about that?

"If you're throwing it away, I quit." The minute I utter the word "quit," I see the advantages. I can leave over a principle. Mom can't object to that.

"Of course you're not quitting. Frannie's coming too," she tells the campers. "Nature will do you good, that's what you need. Start Frannie's engine, kids. No laggers, not even counselors." She whoops a laugh, and Isabel and Pearl drag me by the hands while Gregor pushes from behind as if I were a stalled car.

The Eagles are waiting with Simon at the bottom of the mountain. Did I mention the mountain?

Some people might call it a hill, but it's a dense tangle of trees on a fairly steep slope about a half mile from the barn, and to me it seems like bear country. Simon greets every camper differently—special slaps, high fives, pinkie locks, finger wiggles, digits dancing on palms. He knows endless variations, and all the campers are thrilled: me next, me next, me next. To Rocco, Simon bends down: "Head buzz, buddy." Rocco rubs his hand over Simon's buzz cut.

When he spots me, Simon jabs his fist in my direction. His fist waits there, suspended. Am I supposed to respond? Am I expected to knot my hand into a fist and bang his knuckles? Sensing it's the only way to move off his radar, I comply. We knock knuckles. It's so dumb. I feel ridiculous. Can't he just say hello? Truly he's a hyperkinetic human—perhaps a study should be done of him.

The ENP is putting on socks. Thick white gym socks, and the way she does it, you'd think she is slipping on a pair of sexy fishnet stockings. "Who wants to give me their shoulder?" she purrs. Several boys crowd around. She pretends to lean on two of them to rise from sitting to standing.

"Does anyone mind if I pass on this?" she asks.

"Go ahead, Dawn, there's fresh coffee in the cabin," says Harriet. "Frannie's here—they'll do just fine without you. I'm going to check on two leaky canoes."

As Harriet speeds off, Dawn says, "Purse, please."

Hazel hands over a pink shoulder bag she's been toting.

"Water," Dawn commands.

Brandon, holding a small bottle of Evian, passes it to her.

"Scrunchee."

Pearl, the tiara girl, slides off a red velvet one she's been wearing as a bracelet, and the rest of the girls argue over who gets to carry Dawn's things next.

"Whoever gets to the top, the first boy and the first girl," says Dawn, "gets to be the next clothes carrier. Simon is going to tell me. I'm counting on him." She bestows a wide and glamorous smile on Simon. "Have fun," she calls as she swishes away. "Don't miss me too much."

Simon orders everyone to stand tall, and he inspects. "Okay, looking good. One wiggle and we'll leave." He twitches his butt and shakes his shoulders.

All the campers do the drill.

"How about Frannie? How about a wiggle from Frannie?"

He is one second away from saying, "Move your frannie, Fanny." I sense it. Fact, not opinion: If your name is Frannie, as sure as the sun comes up, one idiot after another is going to think he made up the greatest joke by calling you Fanny.

"Hey, Frannie, give us a wiggle."

I jerk my shoulders twice. God, this is humiliating. It satisfies. (Shocker, he didn't use the "fanny" word). Simon takes off, bounding up the trail, while the kids clamor after, jostling to be the lucky one to hike by his side.

Did I mention that Simon coats his nose and cheeks with thick white sunblock the consistency of mayonnaise? He probably gets easily fried, because his skin is as white as a volleyball. Imagine a volleyball sunburned. I suppose it's to be avoided at all costs. In all aspects he's pale, as if he's been put through the washing cycle too many times. His bristly hair is so wheaty light that it seems colorless, and his little blue bird eyes are nearly transparent, like colored glass. His grin is wide and on the goofy side, with a half-inch space between his front teeth. The better to whistle with. In fact, he frequently puts two fingers in his mouth and blows. You can hear it from one end of camp to the other. He doesn't ring my bells—Jenna's expression. She mainly uses it when we scope out a guy at the mall. Although he might ring yours if you are deeply into pecs and bulging arm muscles, like maybe you fancy a Popeye type. He's not artistic, I'll bet you anything. I can't be into anyone who isn't artistic.

With long strides, he leads the way up the narrow trail. As if conducting a guided tour, he identifies trees and wildflowers—big deal, I know them too, from Mom. Now and then he insists that everyone stop and listen to birds. Robins, a woodpecker, a cardinal, a flock of crows—he knows them by their songs. Maybe he is guessing. Would anyone know the difference?

While initially an easy climb, the trail quickly turns steep and rocky. I grab branches for support and balance. The kids leap along like mountain goats. Wearing flip-flops, I'm at a disadvantage. My feet slide off the rubber soles and my toes cramp trying to grip the thong. It's not my fault that I fall behind and lose sight of the pack. A relief, actually. They can't witness my copious sweat. Salty drops drizzle from my forehead over my nose to my lips. I'm gasping—giant nasal inhales, pants and groans.

Oh, man, I hate hiking.

Dad would have carried on about the sunlight. Bright orangey-yellow streaks pierce the tall pines, creating an unusual optical effect. Anything illuminated—a cluster of wildflowers, a camper, a bunch of twigs—glows with an unearthly halo. Frankly I'm more focused on avoiding the low pointy branches covered with prickly needles. Dad could squeeze through a crowd of porcupines and keep his mind on light. Not me. Ducking under one large limb, I stumble, my ankle twists, and I fall sideways into a clump of ferns. Quite an awkward spill—a sort of pitch-and-crumple—but fortunately, by this time I've fallen so far behind that no one notices. Where I land is comfy and cool, if a bit gross, a damp mossy den studded with gnarled toadstools the size of babies' feet.

Why get up? I have no desire to climb a small mountain. They have to come back this way anyway.

After a horizontal time-out, I sit up and peel back the Band-Aid to examine the splinter. It's days later, but that dream is still alive in my head. The funky hotel room, the carpet tickling my feet, the moment at the window when I scraped my hand. I can still hear Dad's voice like an echo in a canyon growing fainter and fainter.

I wasn't there. I couldn't have been, it's impossible, and yet I'm still there. How did I get this splinter?

I stick the bandage back down to protect it, lie back, and review my time in the barn. There are a ton of instances when it could have happened, no question. As I'm running through the possibilities, I feel ground vibration, hear leaves rustle, the crackle of twigs, and distant chattering voices. They're on their way back. I scramble out of the fern pit and onto the trail. Contemplating the best way to present myself, I decide to lean suavely against a tree.

Simon shows up first, edging backward, instructing campers, "Make sure your foot is secure; give yourself a second to get rooted before you take another step." He breaks off a few branches to clear a wider path, tosses them, and steps off the trail to supervise before he spies me. "Hey there, big feet."

My feet *are* big. Size nine and a half. Has he noticed, or is this simply one more of his many strange greetings? Regardless, my feet suddenly loom, large as swim fins. Besides, they're grimy. Grimy swim fins. Now I do not feel suave. I feel the opposite of suave. As Simon passes, heading south, he dusts the remains of some feather ferns off my shoulder. A startling move. As his hand reaches out, I slap my arms across my breasts, reacting as if he's going to grope me. And then what happens? An innocent dusting—his hand whisks my shoulder and the green fluff flies off.

"While we were kicking butt, Frannie was having a snoozerooni," he calls to the campers.

"She's here, we've found her," Lark trumpets. "She was having a nap."

"Hardly," I maintain coldly. "I was scavenging for unusual ferns."

The kids appear red cheeked and winded, but happy. There are lots of shrieks as the downward slope provides a momentum of its own. They all travel faster than they intend. Rocco, last in line, shows me a lizard he's stashed in his pocket. "See this lizard? It's not a lizard, it's a wizard." As soon as he passes, I . . . well, I intend to bop right down the trail behind them, but I can't actually move. I want to. My brain is sending messages to my feet—at least it's trying—but my feet stay put. The trail looks so steep, so incredibly steep.

I grind my flip-flops into the dirt and try to inch along, but then I hit a protruding root. I can slide out of my flip-flops and step over, but the trail dips sharply right after.

Again I lose sight of the kids, although for a short while I hear squeals as they slip and slide down the slope.

Eventually I'll venture down. Eventually. Right

now I'll take another break. This scenery could be a bunch of jigsaw pieces put together. The trail, the fern bog, the forest of trees in summer bloom. The nearest trunk of a pine begins to fragment— that mossy bit would be a spot of green on an otherwise brown piece, the knot in the oak might appear as curvy lines of gray until two pieces fit together. My foot, digging into the earth for traction, breaks into interlocking jigsaw pieces, some of which have blue knobs where they overlap my jeans or a red stripe, the flip-flop thong. My arms splinter. I feel my head dividing, features fracture— one bit contains an eye and part of my nose, another some shading on my cheek. Humpty-Dumpty sat on a wall.

Don't look at the downward slope, that forbidding downward slope.

I'm going to die.

If I had to draw this, I'd draw two abandoned flip-flops. That suggests a story all right, and not a cheery one.

A big fat horsefly buzzes around. Horsefly bites swell and itch like crazy, but I won't wave it off. Almost any move might send me crashing, a stupendous tumble to the bottom. There I would end, one leg one way, one leg the other, startled and broken like Dad.

The crunch of pebbles and dry twigs—that might signal the approach of a small hungry bear. The top of his head bobs into sight, the buzz cut so flat I could balance a glass on it, then Simon's face freshly coated—a slab of white ointment on his nose and cheeks, even a stripe across his forehead. He's stripped off his shirt—that's a shocker: a flaming pink hairless chest, pulsing pecs. Do pecs actually pulse? I believe I detect throbbing, yes, that's my definite impression. His naked arms look positively sculpted and slick from sweat, and that starts me thinking about how I have big circles of sweat under my arms, I probably smell, and he's undoubtedly noticing.

"Go down on your butt," he says.

I think about that. Trouble is, if I do, I have to sit, and it seems wiser to remain static.

Simon holds out his hand. I release the tree, grab his hand, wobble back and forth, but his grip steadies me, in fact I feel as if I'm being anchored by iron.

"Now sit down," he orders.

I lower myself to the ground.

"And mooch along."

"Mooch?"

"Mooch." I swear I detect the tiniest twitch of his lips indicating that he might be holding a grin in check.

I try an MLS from this pathetic position with Simon the giant hovering above. A waste of energy. "You go ahead," I tell him.

"I'll wait. No big deal."

"Please go on." I guess he hears hysteria in the high-pitched screech that I not too successfully suppress, because he acquiesces.

"You sure?"

"Yes."

When he's out of sight, I begin the mooch, moving my feet first and then my hands, scooting my butt up last. I get good at it, descending faster and faster, even learn to keep my butt elevated so it doesn't get scraped. Just before I hit the home stretch, the path levels to a modest incline. I'm able to rejoin the campers walking. "Hi, there," I call, relieved not to have been humiliated in front of them.

"Fanny came down on her frannie," says Simon. "Let's give her a cheer."

19

What a jerk. Now Rocco is calling me Fanny every five seconds, like I really care, but it's so tedious and inevitable that an uncreative person like Simon would crack the oldest joke in the book, and, as a result, all the way home, Rocco is shouting, "Hey, Fanny, where's your butt?" until his sister nearly pulls his arm out of his socket and Mr. DeAngelo has to stop the bus and squeeze his ample body down the aisle to physically separate them.

Tonight, working the puzzle isn't calming. I'm

too wired. I gnaw red licorice vines while I hunt through the box for blue-and-white pieces. In the photo they appear to be a dinghy floating in the cove. Why would Simon slather sunblock over his face and then let his chest fry? Who cares what the answer to that is?

Boat bits, boat bits. Here's another. Aha, this fits together. What are these coral-and-gray pieces? I start another pile for them. I am surrounded by little heaps of puzzle pieces and a smorgasbord of tasties—vines, peanuts, a bag of chocolate bits, a package of Velveeta. It's hazardous to stretch or shift positions or I'll knock one pile into another. I should have said something squelching to Simon. Something squelching like . . . I don't know, my mind is blank. Lobster. I could have called him lobster, you know, because of how red he is, all sunburned. Well, that would have been a pathetic retort. I'm always trying to relive the moment. What I should have said instead of what I did say, which, in this case, was nothing.

Oops, I pressed a piece of cheese into the puzzle.

I've assembled a blue-and-white–striped row-boat and fragments of deep-blue sea where the puzzle pieces loop outside the boat's edge. In the photo the image seems flat, but when it's put together in the puzzle, I discern the curve of the hull, the shallow interior; I even sense buoyancy. Is there someone in the boat? I look closely. Is that smudge of color a person? Whoops. I slam my hands against the floor to steady myself. What happened?

Did the floor of my room tilt sideways?

No, impossible. I'm tipsy from exhaustion, my balance unstable from leaning over the puzzle, my brain scrambled from hours of scrutinizing the minute differences between colors and between shapes.

At the edge of the room, where carpet meets wall, the floor humps up, and this hump ripples toward and under me, and behind it another appears, and another. My stomach lurches as swells in the carpet lift me up and down. Fear shuts my eyes, my tummy somersaults again and again. An instinct, I pat my hair. How bizarre—it's frizzing. I'm chilly. I need a sweater.

Open your eyes, Frannie. Sometimes, when I'm anxious, I order myself around. Like at Dr. Glazer's, when he's drilling. Breathe, you moron. So open those eyes, Frannie girl.

The first thing I see are my bare feet, instantly recognizable because of the chipped lilac toenail polish, in a shallow puddle of water, and stripes, blue and white. That's the floor, blue, white, shiny, and slick. My cold, naked feet are squeezed between a coil of thick, rough rope and a bundle of fishnet. What's this? I touch a piece of yellow rubber, pick it up. OhmyGod, Velveeta cheese. I don't know what to do, so I flick it over the side. Yes, I toss it overboard, understanding I'm in a boat before I've barely seen enough to know it.

I am the only passenger in this small dinghy, and I am seated on a bench, a wooden plank. The boat bobs, and I bob along with it. An unpleasant tang disturbs my nose. Fish are here. Or else it's just sea flavors carried on a wind that stings my face and seals Dad's shirt to my body.

I'm not really in the ocean, though. Water slaps the sides of the boat as if there are tides and currents, but in fact I'm marooned in a pool of water. Each time the boat bobs up, I spy the weirdly shaped edge of the pool, stubby fingers of water jutting in and out. I'd recognize them anywhere: the knobby ins and outs of puzzle pieces. And beyond that . . . beyond my puzzle island there is no beyond. Around the water's edge, tightly clinging to every in and out, wraps a wall of white. Is it solid or vapor? Could it be void? Void: containing no matter. Empty.

I spot a pinpoint glow, a mini beacon of hope, boring through the white. Maybe out there isn't void, maybe that white is weather. It doesn't look or behave like weather. Even thick fog creeps, rises, and rolls, while this stuff merely *is*. I pray it's weather, because otherwise I don't know how to comprehend my place. What world am I in? What space or time? Twisting around, I find no oars, but hooked onto the boat is a silent outboard engine. Is it dead or off, and does it matter? I can't reach the light anyway—it's beyond the water. What would happen if I motored this boat right off the puzzle? Would I collide with a wall, would I bounce off something soft and woolly, would I evaporate entirely the way my arm appeared to evaporate when I stuck it out the window?

The dot of light comforts from a distance— watching it is hypnotic, and besides, there's nothing else to do. Now, on either side of the yellow spot, there appears a green squiggle as if someone has squeezed paint right out of a tube. The green flattens and more colors appear, streaks of milky pink and red, flecks of black. It's all a murky mess and then it's not.

In tiny but precise relief, the yellow glow of a lamp burns inside a second-story window bordered with green shutters. It's the puzzle window I tumbled into, the window of the ancient Irish house with its rose walls and tiled roof. Like the patch of ocean I'm bobbing in, the house has knobby in-and-out edges. Unmistakably they resemble the unconnected sides of jigsaw pieces.

The way this image revealed itself reminds me of what happened when Mom decided I might need glasses. I couldn't catch the ball at a Little League tryout, and she couldn't accept that I am no athlete. The problem had to be my vision. So she took me to the ophthalmologist, who made me look through gigantic binoculars attached to a big black metal machine. The doctor kept asking, "Can you tell me what that is?" "A fuzzy blob," I answered. He spun some dials, and there they were, a wheel with spokes, a car, a rabbit, a mouse in a cage. Well, there's no doctor here spinning dials; there's only me and my eyeballs on the loose. Trust your eyes, they'll lead you where you need to go. Hope Dad was right about that.

Dad? Dad! I see him in the window. Is it him? From here, barely illuminated, barely more than a silhouette. He raises his arm. It is the way he always greeted me. Whenever I walked out the door at Mom's and he was waiting by the car, he would hold his hand up, flat, fingers spread. "Hey, I'm here, this way, Frannie." As if I didn't know where I was going. As if I wasn't running right at him. Top speed.

"Dad! Dad!" I stand in the boat, raise both arms, and signal wildly. "Dad!"

A wave socks me right out of the boat. My back slaps the water. As I sink, water rushes into my nose and mouth, my shirt balloons.

20

Gagging and sputtering, I'm on my back, rolling side to side on the floor of my room.

"Frannie, are you all right?"

I flip over, shove the puzzle board under the bed, and with my comforter I blanket what remains—my box, piles of sorted pieces. Mom whacks the door wide; it slams into one of the big cardboard boxes and comes right back at her.

"I'm . . ." I can't stop coughing. I have to bend over while she pats my back and I have a complete coughing fit, spitting up water.

"Good grief, what happened? You're all wet."

My clothes are stuck to me, my hair plastered to my head. She's right. I am all wet.

"Why?"

Why?

"Why did you take a shower in your clothes? What's wrong with your foot?" Mom kneels down. "Give me a tissue, would you?" Mel hands one over, and she wipes my foot and examines some yellow goop. Am I excreting strange pus? She smells it. "Cheese?"

"Maybe. Velveeta."

"You're eating in the shower? For God's sake, Frannie, you're shivering, where's your towel? Why did you take a shower in your clothes?" Her voice spikes shrill. She sprints into the bathroom, revealing, behind her, all of Mel in boxer shorts. Not a sight I ever wanted to see. "What are you doing up so late?" He cranks his head from side to side. Loud cracks are heard. Perhaps his knuckles are in his neck. "What time is it?"

My mom sweeps back in, wraps me in a giant towel, and keeps on ranting, "Taking a shower in her clothes. Eating cheese. What is she thinking?"

She. That's me.

"Take off your clothes."

"I can't take them off with him here."

I notice my hand. The Band-Aid hangs. Mom grabs my wrist and we both look closely. "What's wrong here?" she asks.

"Nothing. I had a splinter; it's gone." It *is* gone. It must have been washed out by the water. "Mom, stop fussing."

"What smells?" says Mel.

"I'm fine, I'm really fine." I back them out. "I was painting at camp today, and showering seemed like an easy way to get the paint off my clothes and me at the same time."

"I didn't notice paint on your clothes."

"Why?"

Recognize my trick: Derail them with something nonresponsive. Mel gets a cloudy look, as if he can't read the writing on the medieval walls, but Mom blasts on, "Why is your comforter on the floor?" That one last question remains as I shut the door, almost excising Mom's nose.

Why am I wet?

I drop the towel and peel off my clothes. Why am I wet? How could I be wet?

After wrapping myself up again, I sit on the bed.

Could I be having blackouts?

I heard about them in second grade from Maria. "He drank a fifth," she said, swinging upside down on the jungle gym. "Dad had a blackout." She raised her desktop and stashed her lunch inside. I came home and asked my mom. "What's a fifth? What's a blackout? Maria's dad has them." Mom put it all together and told me what happens if you drink too much liquor. Could a person have a blackout without drinking at all and take a shower they don't remember? Or did I walk in my sleep during a dream and dunk myself?

I tuck the towel around me, scoop up my wet

duds, and carry them into the bathroom. I can't help noticing: The jeans and shirt are sopping, but the shower curtain and tub are dry. No way was I recently in there getting doused. I wring out the wet, squeezing hard, and hook the jeans over the shower spout. What smells? Mel was right—something smells. I mash Dad's shirt to my face. Briny. I sniff the jeans. Briny. I sniff my arm. What smells? Me. I lick my arm. Salt. The water on me is salty. Grabbing a hank of hair, I pull it around. I taste it, smell it, feel it. My hair has been in the ocean. Ocean-wet hair is stiff. When I come home from the beach, my hair has the texture of wood.

I drape Dad's shirt over the tub, taking care to smooth the wet wrinkles before I acknowledge the reality: I was there. I brush my teeth with extra diligence, prolong the chore by doing stupid things like pressing the electric toothbrush on my tongue—a sensation that creeps me out. I even apply a moisturizing lotion that Jenna left months ago, the last time she slept over. Before Dad died.

I pull one of Dad's T-shirts over my head, my sleep outfit.

It seems important to view the night outside my bedroom window, to reassure myself that the moon still occupies its proper place, that the evergreen remains firmly rooted.

When I slide the puzzle from underneath the bed, I know where I am. That helps, because I have to fathom where I've been. I was there. I bobbed in that dinghy. My feet got wrinkly in sea water, sandwiched between a coil of thick rope and a fishing net. As I look at the puzzle, both of these objects are undetectable, mere smudges in the boat's interior. No, the details aren't clear, only the big picture. I accidentally pressed cheese onto a puzzle piece, and the cheese entered the puzzle with me. I tossed the cheese overboard, and somehow it came back out, into this world. Perhaps I thrashed it out when I was sinking.

I was there.

Those fingers of water I spied every time the

boat bobbed up resembled the edges of jigsaw pieces because they *were* the edges of jigsaw pieces. Only life-size.

While I rocked in that boat, the ancient Irish house—the only other section I've completed—revealed itself through the great white mass, whatever bizarre version of nothingness that was. I contemplate both images now, distant from each other on the puzzle board, placed approximately where they would go if the puzzle were completed: striped boat near the bottom right and, center stage, the house with its open window and . . . No. I bend in closer. What's happened here? I angle my desk lamp so the light beams down directly and get close up again. Trust your eyes? In the puzzle, the window is now closed, shutters turned inward. No beckoning glow of light sneaks between the slats.

My dad was there, waving at the open window.

Only now the window's shut.

My dad was there.

I have to think and I have to think clearly, a

challenge when you've got the jitters. I make faces when I'm stressed. Poke my tongue into my cheek or jut out my lower teeth and chomp them repeatedly into my upper lip. *"Charmante"*—Jenna always trots out her few French expressions when she sees my metamorphosis into Frankenstein's monster. Sometimes it helps, it does, to walk around stiff legged, contorting my features. Don't ask me why it helps, I'm clueless.

I dial her number, and she answers on the first ring. "James?" she moans sleepily.

James? I hang up.

Never before has it been anyone but me when her phone rings at this hour. But now it's James the Albert-Waldo phoning after midnight to discuss garlic, or make big smacking kiss noises, or coo a breathy, repulsive "I love you." I don't think that fact should make me cry, but for some stupid reason I have to wipe my eyes.

My phone rings. Obviously she dialed star-six-nine. I turn it off.

Notes, Frannie. Make notes.

I open an old spiral notebook from algebra class and turn to an empty page. *Important Facts*. I write that at the top.

First time. Through the window. But when I tried again, I couldn't do it. That means either: a) a fluke; b) I can't enter the puzzle the same way twice; or c) Jenna was with me and I'm the only one allowed in. I don't know why I think of travel in and out as something that has rules. Maybe it has no rules at all, maybe it's ruleless and I have no control at all. The puzzle will suck me in and toss me out at will.

No control at all? I write that down too.

Second time. In the boat. Even if I could go back in that boat again, I wouldn't want to.

Why did the cheese return with me? Maybe nothing can stay that wasn't originally there, that doesn't belong?

The Great Woolly White. That's what I'm calling void land, the world outside the puzzle. What is it?

"Frannie, are you still awake?"

I kill the light. "Going to sleep right now. Night, Mom."

Fortunately she doesn't come padding down the hall.

Somewhere in my closet is a flashlight. I sidle around the room, steering clear of furniture and boxes. As soon as I shut myself inside the closet, I wave my hand around until it collides with the overhead string, then tug it to light the place. Unfortunately my closet is a big pigsty. I plow through old shoes, backpacks, stray mittens, Rollerblades that I could never learn to skate on, ditto a skateboard, comic books, piles of plastic rollers and other hair equipment like old brushes and a dead blow dryer, gross. I push aside a sleeping bag and finally find the flashlight.

A slow sweep of the beam across the puzzle board unveils each possibility, abandons it, suggests another: the dome of a church, a section of rocky cliff (the edge where rock meets sky), a couple of roofs assembled to suggest the houses they belong to, part of a stone wall. Zigzagging the light over the floor, I locate the carved box. Discovered in darkness, as if unearthed from hidden recesses, the box assumes its true identity, a treasure chest. No gold or rubies but a fortune so much dearer: It brought me back my dad.

I remove the top to get the photo, protected now by a Baggie, sandwiched-sized.

Using my flashlight, I compare the photo image to the partial bits in progress on the board. What's the best route back in?

I'm not putting myself on any rocky cliffs—my disastrous hike at camp was enough uphill and downhill for life. Roofs without houses—that doesn't seem sensible. The church dome has a narrow balcony that wraps it, but as yet no church to support it. The church towers over the village, and the dome is the highest point. It was scary enough to be stranded in a dinghy surrounded by the Great Woolly White, but to end up perched on a narrow balcony, where with one false move, I might fall into the GWW (my lovely legs scissored as if I had executed a really bad dive)—that prospect is terrifying.

That leaves the stone wall.

According to the photo, there are several stone walls. The one along the shore is a safe location, perfect for a touchdown, but another stone wall along the side of the mountain is the worst of all places to find myself. These pieces I've put together so far could belong to either.

What am I going to do?

As I wonder in near darkness, my eyes drift to a mound of jigsaw pieces illuminated by a circle of light—all of them mixtures and hues of coral and gray—one of many piles of sorted pieces around the edge of the puzzle board. What's weird—no, mind-boggling—is that the flashlight in my hand is not pointed in that direction. My arm's hanging by my side, and the flashlight, held loosely, points at an empty spot on the carpet. The carpet should be lit up. There should be a bright circle of fuzzy green, but there's not. The direction of the flash-light and its circle of light have no relationship. They've parted company. I jerk the flashlight over, pointing at the coral-and-grays, to correct the mis-take. I don't know why I do that. It's instinct to use my source to capture the light—as if such a thing were possible, how absurd to try, and yet it works. When I move the flashlight again, the circle of light stays with it, once more in my control. I test the flashlight, looping curlicues, a treble clef across the wall, and arc the light back down. Where does it land? The coral-and-gray pieces.

What will these be when I put them together?

I have to study the photo again. Fortunately the flashlight beam cooperates, making me wonder if that light displacement really did happen. Near the church there's an orange house . . . No, some of these coral-and-grays have knobby ends tipped with dark green, and nothing around this orange house matches that. These pieces must compose this section in the hills beyond the town. What is it?

Some sort of long, low building? A garden abuts— that could be the dark green. Those might be stone steps, a route down to the house where I spotted Dad. Steps, that's good, not too treacherous.

Before immersing myself in making matches, I prepare. I have no control, I remind myself, falling in and ejecting out. It could happen at any time. I dress in cargo pants, my own shirt, a sweater tied around my waist, clunky boots with serious treads. I'm not ending up in Ireland barefoot, bare-assed in Dad's big shirt.

It's one in the morning and I'm wired. The possibility of Dad is a caffeine jolt of epic proportions. I'm possessed. Determined. There is nothing braver, fiercer, and more glorious than the tiny ember of hope burning in my heart.

21

Rewarding me instantly, I get a match with the first two pieces I try. For the next two hours I am so focused that I can memorize the bumps on a jigsaw piece, keeping the visual in my brain while I unerringly locate the one that completes it. Wielding the flashlight proves an impediment—I like having both hands free. I move my desk lamp to the rug and adjust the arm. The beam hits my group of similar-colored puzzle pieces but in no way brightens up the room enough to attract my mom's attention.

The coral color, which appears to be primarily the structure's wall, glows so vividly in spots that it seems as if there are lights behind it. Is it transparent? The gray, a roof, may be an awning; its edges appear to ripple as if buffeted by a wind. Another piece snaps in. I love this. I love that a small, utterly abstract piece joins with another and something real is born. If some abstract art can be described as stripping down an image to its essence, then "puzzling" is the opposite. Here I'm moving from abstract to concrete. Very cool. Dad would get that. Maybe he gets that. Maybe he knows. Present tense. Dad knows.

Lou, lou, skip to my lou. My mom used to dance around the room with me and sing that song. Before Mom and Dad separated. I remember she danced me outside and swung me into the air, once, twice, three times, and into his arms. He was washing the car, his arms were all soapy, and he put a dab of suds on my nose. Lou, lou . . . a final piece clicks in. I definitely discern blurs behind the wall—wispy shadows that must be people. Are they? I lean closer.

An old woman's face peers into mine. Shrewd black eyes, thick black brows flecked with gray that meet and greet over her nose, a mole on her cheek. She frowns and wipes her hands on a white cloth that hangs from her waist. All in black. Except for that cloth, she's dressed in black.

Is she Death?

That's crazy. I am so crazy. Death isn't a woman.

Death isn't even a person, and if it were, it wouldn't have a dishtowel hanging from its waist. I doubt if Death's eyebrows would need tweezing either. I sense that this woman is seriously efficient and I'm holding her up for some reason.

She speaks. I can't understand a word she says.

She leans closer. I lean backward.

A chair. I'm in a chair. There's a red carnation on the table. My mom is anti-carnation. They're tacky, she told me, and if she used them in bouquets, she'd be out of business. This carnation, this single stem in a glass bud vase, confirms absolutely that I am no longer at home.

I'm in the puzzle again.

The woman's hair is short—gray and wavy, sprayed to stiffness. Jenna's mom says that "going gray" is "going to seed." She told Jenna that if it came down to eating or dying her hair, she'd pick dye. Hardly any women in Hudson Glen have gray hair, but I bet that Ireland is full of gray-haired grandmas. I wonder if she's a relative. So not Death. Maybe a relative.

Fortunately, I didn't inherit any big moles like that.

Wires are crossed. That's the sound I hear, the drone of interference, and as it gets louder, it softens into the hum of conversation, and in spite of the fact that a possible relative is waiting for me to answer a question I don't understand, I look around.

I'm in a restaurant, a cheery place that Dad would like. "No affect, Frannie." That's what he would say, meaning nothing fancy. Plastic patio furniture, a checkerboard floor of tan-and-white tiles. Strings of tiny lights, hung like garlands, twinkle on the ceiling. Pretty lights in the palest orange. Coral. Of course, coral. The ceiling itself is a striped gray awning. Coral and gray. People around me chatter and eat, and I can't understand a word they say. My hand rests on an oilcloth. Only it's not oil-cloth, it just feels like oilcloth from Dad's studio. In fact it's a tablecloth, plastic coated for easy wiping, as a busboy demonstrates, swiping a sponge across it.

I'm sitting at a table and an old woman with stiff hair and a stiff shiny black dress is talking to me in a language I don't understand.

The busboy lays a placemat in front of me. A white paper placemat with scalloped edges.

At the next table a woman points at her plate. *"Troppo salato, troppo salato,"* she scolds a waiter, and the lady in black who is failing to communicate with me rustles over, takes her plate, hands it to the waiter, and waves him away. This woman works here. She might be the boss.

This restaurant, an outdoor patio, is sheltered and protected on three sides by sheets of heavy plastic. The fourth wall, solid, has a swinging door through which waiters, balancing multiple plates, glide in and out. This wall, painted with grape vines, tweaks my memory. Rendered in thick broad strokes, the vines meander like country roads. Fat bunches of green and purple grapes, outlined in black, remind me of drawings in a child's coloring book. Maybe one of mine from when I was five. That could be it. They're tucked away in my sub-conscious along with the flavor of strained carrots.

Is my dad here?

I spring up. My eyes bounce from table to table, searching the room. A young girl sticks a rose in my face. It's so startling, I can't respond. The flower girl, no more than eight years old, cradles several red roses, each wrapped in cellophane. When I'm apparently struck dumb by a rose, she leaves me, goes to a table, and offers them there. They shoo her off.

Not here. Not now, anyway. Dad's not here.

"Troppo salato." The disgruntled woman complains again, although her dinner has been whisked away, and she consoles herself adjusting her bust, wiggling and lifting large breasts in a silky dress that coats her skin like syrup, then letting them settle. The man with her is performing surgery on a fish, carefully lifting out a perfectly intact backbone, admiring it for a second before he lays it down. He's far too busy with his fish to appreciate that she is not just having dinner with him, she and her breasts are keeping him company.

I wonder if James is more interested in fish than Jenna's breasts.

The woman's hair is swept on top of her head into a curly pile. Looks like a shrub. No kidding, Mom could pass off that head topping as an azalea. With a gentle pat the lady assures herself that the "do" is still in place. I take in all the hairstyles. Her dinner partner—slim, handsome, and exotically dark skinned—has jet-black hair, parted on the side and combed over flat. What sort of product has he used? I can see the comb marks clearly. It's as if his hair has been tilled. A lady twirling pasta has a cap of tight gray curls inspired by local sheep. Aren't there sheep in Ireland? Another woman has a raven-colored mane twisted into a snail-like concoction and stabbed with a tortoiseshell comb.

The styles are not as old as the town. But practically.

The woman with the snail-shaped twist ceremoniously devours oysters on the half shell, raising each shell as if for public viewing before tilting her head back and letting the oyster slide down her throat. She dabs her lips with a white napkin and selects another oyster, holds it up, and sees me watching. Abruptly she sets the shell back on the plate. Her eyes lock on mine, and then, like a virus that spreads from table to table, people stop slurping oysters, forking penne, twirling spaghetti, filleting fish, sipping wine, and turn their heads my way.

They know I don't belong here.

I am definitely science exhibit A—I feel gigantic, misshapen, two headed as I weave between tables and dodge waiters, searching for the way out. USCITA. There is a sign. That must be the name of the restaurant. Or does it mean bathroom? Am I headed for the bathroom? The woman in black jabbers at me when I pass. What is she saying, why don't I understand anyone? I see another sign with the same name, USCITA. There's an opening, a seam in the plastic wall. A way out.

Pushing aside the plastic, I enter a swirling mist. Whirls of fog wrap me up and blind me, then unwind and breeze off, leaving behind a trail like a jet stream. In the sudden clearness, I spy a stone wall webbed with moss and ivy before I'm enveloped again, and this time the fog just sits on me. "Hello." I toss a greeting into nothing. I can see my hand when I hold it in front of my eyes, but as I lower my hand, it fades, as if covered with gauze, then disappears altogether. Nope, no hands, and no feet either, thanks to this soup. I stay put. No way am I hip-hopping around in fog as blinding as the wrapping on a mummy; who knows what I'll crash into. A strip of fog peels off, then another. They dance like streamers—does someone have them by the tail, is someone rippling them with the snap of a wrist? It's a shimmery sight, because in between the ribbons of fog are ribbons of life, which I try to assemble into one image. A wall here, there, too? Lots of leafy green. Red flowers. The sightings are disorienting—the glimpses are too brief, the images too wiggly. I can't be sure what they are or how they fit together, and then mercifully the fog thins and spreads to an even film and the world stops gyrating. Through a fine, fine mist like fairy dust, I can see where I am.

An ancient garden paved with rough uneven stones. Here and there, big terracotta pots boast geraniums so fat and lush and laden with red blooms that Mom might have been here dumping in packets of plant food by the dozen. The high walls veined with moss and ivy are crude, rocky patchworks. There are two of them, one to my left and one to my right. Behind me the restaurant glimmers a soft amber behind the protective plastic, and directly ahead is a lagoon from which the fog rises like steam. Perhaps it's a hot spring.

Jenna's mom once went to a hot spring. In order to be in constant communication with her office, she'd gotten a BlackBerry. For weeks she did nothing but walk around the house with her head down punching that BlackBerry. We nicknamed her BlueBerry. We were hoping that one week relaxing at a hot spring might cure her addiction (and neck). So did Jenna's dad; her housekeeper, Alice; and probably even Mambo. But when BlueBerry came home, she was still obsessed. Finally Jenna's dad threw the BlackBerry in the garbage disposal, mangling it, and her mom and dad had a fight, screaming, slamming doors. Jenna was scared. We stayed on the phone the whole time, and she asked, "What's divorce like, really?" and I said it wasn't a big deal, which was a big lie. I said the worst thing was that you had to travel from one house to another, but that was another big lie. The worst is that your family is gone, dead and buried, so even though you still have a mom and still have a dad, your family is history.

You worry about your parents, too, that they're okay . . . and you work hard to make them happy. I don't know why, but you do. (I know it doesn't seem like I try to make Mom happy. It might even seem like I try to make her miserable, but that's a post-Mel development.) The arrival of Mel meant I could go from trying to make her happy because maybe her life was wrecked to thinking that she was trying to wreck my life. The point is, divorce means your parents are on your mind. One way or another, they loom.

But anyway, I didn't tell any of this to Jenna, and fortunately her parents made up, and BlueBerry got another BlackBerry, but she agreed to stop using it after seven at night.

I inch to the edge of the steamy pool, expecting to see bubbling water beckoning me in for a dip, but the lagoon is empty, a crater breathing forth smoky mist.

Keeping safely back, I skirt the rim. It curves, then hooks sharply, and I find myself at the tip of a skinny finger of land no wider than the length of an arm. Dusky air billows up the front and sides. I don't want to look into the pit again—it seems perilous; at the same time, I'm compelled to sneak a peek. No bending over, no risky neck extensions. I try to get a gander at what's down there by angling my eyeballs southward. The crater's edge is jagged, stones shaved and broken as if the person paving it got fed up and didn't finish the job. How easy it would be for some rock to come unglued—pressure from a size–nine-and-a-half foot in this clunky boot could do it—and I would plummet in.

As I retreat to safer ground, taking baby steps,

the air churns again with intermittent powdery blasts that dissipate in seconds. I hear murmurs. A man's low voice, a woman's giggle. Then they're silent and I notice the quiet, really absorb the utter absence of noise. This busy air that thins and thickens, swirls and blinds, is soundless. No whoosh, whirr, or whistle. No rasp of ivy against stone or flutter of those red geranium blossoms. The plants don't move at all. Why isn't there wind, if there's all this swirling action? My shirt hangs as limp as it would on a still day. Hedge hair doesn't ruffle either. More giggling.

Something about the giggles makes me cautious. I don't know why. "Who's there?" I whisper. Another fit of giggles. With the crater belching dragon breath on my right, and on my left a high stone wall, I cautiously proceed in the direction of the noise, and soon begin a downward trek on steep stone steps. I take each one sideways because the drop, at least a foot, requires a routine: balance on one foot, deep knee bend as I reach down to the lower step, bring second foot down, and straighten up. Begin again. Each time the first foot lands, the impact sends a jolt up my thigh. Between cursing and concentrating, I don't see them until we virtually collide.

A man dressed in gray and tan is camouflaged against the rock. As far as I can tell, he has no idea I'm here. He faces the wall. With his arm raised, using his hand to brace himself, he's created a little alcove where, judging from more giggles, a woman is happily trapped. I can't help myself, I stare. Of her I spy only some limbs: her pale naked calves between his trousered legs, one arm dangling, her fingers looped around the thin strap of a small patent leather purse.

The man pivots slightly as he presses against her. Beside him, a plume of mist curls upward. What is that? Where's it coming from? His jacket. Is it smoke? "Fire," I start to shout but slap my hand against my mouth because he pivots more. The lake of billowing mist widens, I now see, and cuts across the steps and up the wall. Up the wall? How is that possible? How could this hole in the ground continue up the wall? How could it take a chomp right out of a man's back? Because that's what it does. His shoulder is there, his hips are intact, but a piece of his back as big as my fist is just plain missing where the crater invades it. Seemingly oblivious, the man continues romancing the woman.

I reach down and, when I feel the solidness of stone, let my body sink. As my knees bend yet again, I lose balance and my butt hits the step with a thump, but none of this disturbs my view or attracts the man's attention. I sit there transfixed. Eventually the man becomes landscape, his body blends in with the rocks, misty fumes from the cove in his back mix with the cloudy air.

Below me there's nothing. The crater eats the steps, the jagged edge bites into them like shark teeth. I don't have the energy to retreat. I need to be horizontal. I do.

Turning sideways, I stretch out. The step is

narrow; the stone riser tight against me provides the unpleasant sensation of being laid out in a sarcophagus. Definition: stone coffin.

Above me, visibility zero. Can't land a plane in a grainy haze. *The blues are hardest. Save the blues for last.* Under me the stone softens to my curves, and I twist a half-turn, tugging my pillow more snugly under my neck. I'm in bed.

22

I keep my eyes on Mel, waiting for the right moment. He lays his six vitamins on the counter next to a glass of orange juice, drops two slices of rye bread in the toaster, then switches his attention back to the coffee maker, scooping in eight spoonfuls, then closing up the smart glossy bag, making sure the twists at the top are secure so his beloved Colombian coffee that he orders over the Internet stays absolutely fresh.

"Uscita," I say.

He flicks the switch on the coffee maker, opens

one cabinet to get the sugar-free jam and granola and another to get his bowl. He has a favorite bowl, like a little kid, blue ceramic. Now that he has all his breakfast parts lined up and ready to salute, he begins assembling.

"Uscita." I throw it out louder, making a stab at the pronunciation. The first time I said, "Us-see-ta," and I accented the back end. This time, "Oo-chee-ta." I put the emphasis on the middle. Who knows how it's pronounced?

"Are you talking to me?" he asks, astonished.

"Yes."

He shoves the spoon into the jam jar and stands there. "It's just that you never do. What did you say?"

"Uscita." This time I chime the syllables, each in a different tone but with equal emphasis— "us-kee-ta."

"I'm sorry. Should I know what that means? Is it a rock group?"

He doesn't have a clue either.

I filter the Cheerios through my fingers, searching for tiny gnats. "I made it up."

He nods as if that makes sense, grateful for my first attempt at conversation, even if it is gibberish. Resuming his morning ritual, he crowds all his pills onto his palm, smacks them flat-handed into his mouth, and gulps a swallow of juice. I find this daily one-gulp downing of six different-colored vitamins, some as large as a potato bug, daring and a little wild.

"Is there an Irish language?" I ask.

"Irish. That's what it's called. Or Gaelic. The Celts, who spoke it, colonized Ireland in 600 B.C. Even though the island was invaded by the Vikings and subsequently by the English, and the primary language is now English, people in Ireland think of Irish as their native language. It's taught in the schools."

More than I need to know. Surprise. Mel could bore the icing off a cake. Besides, I know about Celts. Dad mentioned the Celts a million times—

my box is carved with Celtic knots. I just didn't realize they still spoke the ancient language. "I bet there are some fishing villages where they still speak only Irish."

"Probably. Why?"

"Why what?" Holding a Cheerio to my eye, I try to see through it.

"Why do you want to know about Ireland?"

"Did you sleep well?" I inquire.

Mel is way too curious, but my attempt to reroute him backfires. "Yes," he says, after a long pause, and during this time I can see the wheels spinning in his brain. I see all the serfs jumping into a moat, leaving only *moi* on the bridge to the castle. Frannie is being nice. What is going on? "Why are you interested in Ireland?" he repeats.

"Someone from camp is from there."

"That boy."

Might as well use Simon. He called me Fanny, I can call him Irish. I shrug.

"Is it also because of your dad? He was Irish."

I'm not discussing Dad with Mel.

"So you're half Irish."

Duh. I pass on that, too. I hobble to the refrigerator.

"What's wrong?"

My legs. They are so sore that the muscles in my calves are twanging. As for my left hip, when I sat down, I swear it screamed *no*. Why didn't I realize this before? I mean, I realized it but didn't. On the stairs this morning I was crippled with pain, but I guess I dismissed it as general exhaustion, a side effect of sleeping in boots. As I massage my hip, the pain travels south. I follow it, kneading, until I locate a sore spot where my hip and leg join up. "I hiked at camp," I tell Mel, but the second I say it, I know that doesn't begin to explain it. At camp I'd pooped out after a short ascent, lolled in moss, and returned on my butt. Hardly exertion. This trauma is clearly linked to that steep descent: plunge, squat, straighten, stone step to stone step. Even in recall I feel the shudder.

"What?" says Mel.

"What? Nothing." He caught me drifting, mulling my strange adventure.

"Do you want to see a doctor?"

"I'm fine. Just creaky." I open the milk and sniff. Is it fresh? Hard to be sure. Tilting the container to get a drop on my finger, I overshoot the mark. Milk runs over my hand onto the counter.

"In the Middle Ages there was a job called taster. The person tasted all the food first so the lord of the castle didn't get poisoned. That's what you need," says Mel.

"You can be my taster."

He bursts into laughter—a laugh that rolls and rolls and rolls until it peters out into a sigh. There is something sad about how happy I make him by cracking a lame joke. I concentrate on wiping up the milk, swiping the sponge across the counter. I swipe again more slowly, noting the arc of my arm across the countertop, the sponge in my hand.

"Your bus is here," he tells me.

I'm thinking about the busboy, wiping the table, laying down the placemat.

"It's honking, Frannie."

I am in the bus, munching a granola bar, with Barbie One sitting behind me braiding my hair, when I tap Mr. DeAngelo on the shoulder and instruct him to let me out. Right here, at the gas station coming up, I'll call my mom, I have a sudden and terrible toothache. When he resists—he's not allowed to drop a person off willy nilly—I remind him that I'm not a camper but a counselor. I am not his charge, so he swings the bus into self-serve. Barbie One refuses to release my pigtail, but I pry off her hand, get out, and phone Jenna.

Unfortunately, I have to wait for her and James in the ladies' room, which stinks. I can't risk hanging around the pumps—one of Mom's friends might arrive to fill up. A dashed-off e-mail—subject "Your Daughter"—and Mom would know I'd skipped out on my job.

As soon as they pick me up, I leave a message for

Harriet that I have a toothache. I'll be in tomorrow.

"Why did I hold my nose when I left the message for Harriet?"

Jenna giggles. "I don't know."

"I think I got my nose mixed up with my teeth. You don't sound clogged when you have toothache, do you?"

"What do you think, James?" Jenna walks her fingers across his shoulder and pokes his neck, as if her finger is doing a high kick. From the backseat, I have an unobstructed view of the finger stroll.

"No," says James. "Although you might if your mouth was swollen."

I didn't want him to come along, but as Jenna pointed out, otherwise who would drive? He clutches the wheel with both hands and cranes his head forward like maybe he's checking out the front fender or searching for stray babies crawling across the road. He drives in gasps, frequently hitting the brake for no apparent reason. Jenna sits sideways so she can admire him and talk to me.

"James made osso bucco last night."

"Wow, that's great."

"I wasn't that happy with the quality of the meat," says James.

"What was it?" asks Jenna.

"Shank."

Her brow furrows, as if she's pondering . . . as if she has an opinion about shanks . . . as if, after serious consideration, she's going to recommend another piece of cow for osso bucco.

"But you're a vegetarian," I remind her.

"Not anymore, she's not," James says. "There was marbling in the meat."

"I loved it. I thought it was perfect." She offers me limp, oily, red things from a plastic container. "Sun-dried tomatoes, want one? They're totally delicious."

"No, thanks."

While we're stopped at a light, she pinches one between her fingers and feeds it to James. At least I assume that when she dangles it in front of his face, his tongue shoots out and she drops it on. From the backseat, I'm spared that sight. "Mmm," Jenna says, although he's the one eating. Then her hand pops up with a napkin, which he takes, uses to wipe his mouth, crumples, and hands back to her.

I peek over the seat. They have a picnic. A bottle of water, sun-dried tomatoes, cocktail napkins, and biscotti, which Jenna now offers, and I accept.

When we finally arrive at Dad's (after stopping at Starbucks because James needs an espresso), the place looks unfortunate. Curly moss has grown wild, more pasture now than front yard. The FOR SALE sign has a SOLD slapped across it.

"Frannie, who bought your dad's house?"

"I don't know. I didn't know it was sold."

"Do you want me to wait?" asks James.

"If you don't, how will we get home?"

"I mean, do you want me to come with you?" He hunts through the biscotti bag.

"Oh, sorry. No."

"We'll be right back. Won't we be right back?" Jenna appeals to me.

I nod.

"No problem, Pickle." He selects a biscotti, eyes it from both sides, and crunches while Jenna explains, "He likes them crisp, almost burned."

Severely sore muscles cause me to moan as I unfold from the car and attempt to straighten up. I do not quite make it to vertical. Jenna watches. "What's wrong with you, Frannie?"

I wave her off—it's not worth discussing—and pull her around to the back of the house. It's unbelievable how much my hip aches. "Isn't he sweet? Isn't he just the sweetest," she crows while I walk as if I'm wooden. "Weren't we wrong about him?"

I locate the key hidden under the shingle, but Jenna grabs my hands. Her eyes beseech me. "Frannie, don't you like him? Wasn't that considerate of him to ask?"

"To ask what?"

"If we wanted him along. That practically makes me cry."

"He called you Pickle."

"I know."

"Isn't he into Italian food?"

"So?"

"It's the same thing as the rosemary and à la mode." I angle the padlock to insert the key more easily. Jenna holds it steady.

"I don't get what you're saying. God, this lock is heavy. James is so strong. I think it's from chopping or carrying around iron skillets. You should try to squeeze his biceps. I hope he's not mad at me."

The key clicks. I lift off the padlock and we enter the studio. Above the drafting table, next to Dad's paintbrushes, the wall is bare. "It's gone."

"What?"

"That watercolor. Don't you remember the little painting of grapes?"

"I never knew those were grapes. Do you think he's mad at me?"

"Why would he be mad at you? Jenna, this is important. The painting was on paper with scalloped edges, the size of a placemat. I think it *was* a placemat—that was why Dad liked it. I'm sure that's why he liked it—because it was a painting on a placemat." I examine the wall. "It was here, I can tell it was here." I show her the holes where the pushpins were stuck.

"I remember the painting, Frannie, but are you sure those were grapes? I thought they were little balloons." Jenna sits in Dad's chair and spins.

"Jenna, don't."

"What?"

"It seems weird, your spinning in his chair."

She grasps the drafting table to stop herself. "Sorry." She starts to handle some paintbrushes, then catches herself. "I hope he's not mad."

"Why would James be mad?"

"Usually when I tickle his neck, he takes my hand and kisses it. Sometimes he says, *'Bellissima.'*"

"Bellissima?"

"'Beautiful' in Italian."

"Well, I was in the backseat, maybe he didn't want me to throw up. Jenna, listen, this is serious. This is life or death."

"Sorry."

"Stop saying sorry. It makes me crazy. Those were grapes. They were all watery, kind of impressionistic, and it wasn't anything Dad normally liked because it was pretty—he was always carrying on about how great art wasn't sweet or pretty, it didn't remind you of lollipops or lambs, it should shock or jar you."

"What's that mean?"

"I know what it means."

"Are you sure?"

"I understood my dad, okay? He liked that watercolor because it was on a placemat—remember how he loved the Laundromat that not only had washing machines, but also sold red velvet cake, and the mobile phone store with a manicurist?—but they were definitely grapes and they reminded me—"

"Of what?"

"Last night, in the puzzle—"

"In the puzzle?"

"I was in the puzzle, Jenna. That's why I can't walk. I had to hike down steep stone steps. I've been in three times."

She seizes my shoulders and shakes me. "Frannie. Tell me, you've got to tell me everything."

I push her away and duck under the table.

"What are you doing?"

"Looking for the drawing." I crawl around, move stacks of newspapers, and feel behind things. Dust. Cobwebs. An old fork. Stray nails. No painting. Jenna has to assist when I try to stand. "This is awful. It was here when I came with my mom. Maybe the person who bought the house stole it."

"Frannie, how did you get in the puzzle? How could it have happened? That's impossible."

"I know, but it happened."

"Frannie, no."

"Yes. I can't believe that painting's gone."

"You're absolutely positive that you didn't have another dream?"

"Last night I swear I was there twice."

"Where?" James strolls in.

"Nowhere. Nothing. It's not here."

"What isn't here?" he asks.

"Nothing, we're done, let's go."

While I'm locking up, Jenna throws me pleading looks. When you've been friends forever, you don't need words to get the message: eyes so wide they're pulsing coupled with the tiniest jerk of the head toward James. Finally we're in the car ahead of James, and in those two seconds before he opens the door and slides behind the wheel, she explodes, but in a whisper, "Can't we tell him?"

"No."

He sticks the key in the starter. I wait for the sound of the motor. Nothing. I stretch my neck to get a view into the front. He's just sitting there. James the Albert-Waldo might be waiting for a herd of goats to cross the road. "What's going on?"

he asks. "Is this about me?"

"It's not about you," says Jenna. She throws me another desperate look.

"Okay, I'll tell you, but you have to keep a secret."

"James is so great at that."

"Actually, I am," he says.

23

He opens the refrigerator, tunnels through. "Aha." He unearths a plastic container. "Ricotta."

"Cheese," Jenna tells me.

He pops off the top, sniffs, and sighs. Jenna checks to see if I'm digging him. He opens the crisper, dives in, and surfaces with a bunch of weeds that he waves under my nose. "Parsley, dill." Out comes a lemon." He closes the crisper with his knee, extracts a box of eggs from the top shelf, and asks Jenna to "grab that half and half, and take two eggs out of this." He shoves the egg box into her arms.

"What are you making?" she inquires.

"Ricotta tart."

Jenna looks my way, chin tucks down, eyebrows rise. Translation: I hope you heard that, I hope you're impressed.

"Cut this in half." He hands her a lemon. "You relax, Frannie." He cracks the eggs and empties them one-handed, selects a whisk from a host of kitchen doodads, and starts beating. "You should always eat when you unburden your heart."

Jenna's eyebrows nearly fly off her forehead. I pull a long face, dittoing "impressive" in our silent conversation, but frankly I think James read that line somewhere and is quoting. What normal guy says that?

"James's parents are never home," says Jenna.

"Never home," James echoes.

"His little brother's at day camp. His mom and dad own a hardware store in Cold Spring, and they work all day." Jenna does a split. The kitchen's a galley, and when she sinks down and raises her arms, each hand proffering a half lemon, she pretty much takes up the space.

James accepts the lemon from his balletic assistant and, with one twist of each half, squeezes the juice into the eggs. He's in constant motion. He may be awkward and gangly to the point that no limb appears to be aware of another when he lopes around in regular life, he may drive a car in fits and starts as cautious as a canary in fear of a cat, but here in the kitchen he's as graceful as Jenna: reaching for this and that, sometimes simultaneously, spinning from one spot to another, deftly slicing/dicing/whipping. The fish has found water, or maybe the octopus has: He beats the cheese into the eggs with one hand while he reaches for a glass with another and knocks a lower cabinet closed with his foot. Signor Waldo the Italian chef has another moniker now: Octopus Man.

He works with total concentration. His teeth seem less rabbit size even with his mouth hanging open; his normally placid eyes flash. Must be, yes, I spot it: passion. I remember Dad in his studio. The excitement, the lack of awareness of other people, total immersion.

Lunch was James's idea. When I warned him, "It's a long story," and Jenna injected, "It's amazing, James, totally amazing, wait until you hear," that's when he suggested that we all hang out at his place.

While his sous chef rubs suggestively against him every time she wiggles past in the narrow kitchen, I hang in the breakfast nook. Out the window, the parking lot is something I might draw: endless asphalt striped with white, one car with its hood up parked crazily across two spaces. A pizza box discarded nearby.

Looking at this vision of dullness (rife with suggestion), I could doubt my last night's adventure, doubt it utterly, were it not for my tortured calves, pinging thighs, and a hip that wants to cry. Simon's naked chest, sun-splotched pink, invades my ruminations. I wonder if he's peeling. I even get a vision of him scraping away dead skin with his thumbnail. Jenna tugs my sleeve. "Frannie, look."

James's knife chatters across the wooden board as he mows down parsley. "Mincing," she boasts.

Soon we all settle down together while the tart bakes. I have to begin at the beginning, for James's sake. He keeps refilling wineglasses with lime zingers (lime and club soda) so sour my lips shrivel, but they do go extremely well with olives and some tasty glop he calls red-pepper paste. Jenna listens avidly, as if she's never heard any of my tale before. When I get to the boat episode, new to her, she squeezes my arm for encouragement and sometimes from excitement. The incredulities mount, I'm painfully aware, even though this time I don't embroider, not one bit. When I get to splashdown, my chest is so tight with anxiety that I rush through it: "Then I'm on the floor of my bedroom, soaked, flailing, coughing up saltwater—saltwater, I swear. My mom can tell you that I was sopping wet, if you want to ask. But the tub and shower were dry, so then I knew there was no way, absolutely no way that I dreamed or imagined it."

"I believe you totally," says Jenna instantly.

We wait for James. He picks some olive between his teeth.

"You don't believe me? You don't buy any of this, do you? You think I'm crazy."

"No he doesn't," Jenna assures me while I bet she's kicking him under the table.

"Can I believe you and not believe you?" he asks finally.

"What's that supposed to mean?"

"Well, it's weird, you know."

I have to admire that. I really do. Let's face it. If someone unloaded those tales on me, I'd want to cart O Delusional One to the nearest looney bin, but James is cool with me. It is weird, but he's listening; that's fair. I feel secure enough to ramble on about the GWW, how it tucked and turned around the edges of the water when I was in the puzzle, about the next trip in—the restaurant, the waterless lagoon (that crater) belching smoke in the ancient garden. All sorts of thoughts fall out as I try to make sense of things, impose logic on madness. "When I studied the puzzle this morning, I realized that I hadn't completed the garden. I fell into the puzzle too soon. That crater wasn't a crater. It was the missing part of the puzzle, and the jagged edge, well, it would be jagged because puzzle pieces end arbitrarily. I bet one missing piece had a little knob right where that man's back was. That why he had 'crater back.' I mean, the guy was missing his lower back, but he was still smooching away." I gulp some zinger, forgetting that a little goes a long way. My insides contract.

As I rant about the restaurant and the garden,

James shifts in his seat, scratches his neck, and wings his elbows back. Finally he spikes a fork into the red pepper paste, so it stands straight up as if he's stuck a flag in the moon, claiming it for America. I stop. "Now you really don't believe me, right?"

There's a pause long enough for a flower to wilt.

"Well, it's weird," he says again.

Jenna titters from nervousness—I think it was her, but it might have been me. A little laughter begets more—and more. Soon we're stomping around the kitchen in pain holding our stomachs, trying to stop. I'm gasping, protesting it really is true, and Jenna holds up her hands to push the giggles away, and James sighs against the counter, overcome, until finally, it all dies out, and what's left is awkwardness.

I can't help myself, I have to fill it. "My dad's there, I know he is."

No one contradicts me.

"The tart's almost ready," says James.

"It smells fabulous," says Jenna.

James gets some salad greens out of the refrigerator, tosses in some pine nuts, and slices in slivers of pear. After mixing oil and vinegar right into the salad, and tasting a leaf, he puts on two oven mitts, boxes Jenna's ears with them, and slides the tart out of the oven and onto the counter. With a flick of his hands, both mitts fly off. He taps the tart with his finger. "Perfect."

"Isn't he hot?" Jenna mouths.

I'm starting to sweat. I drank out of a glass. I scooped red pepper paste onto a cracker, but I used the cracker to do it. Now I have to use a fork and a plate. Jenna hands them out.

"Were these in the dishwasher?" I could ask. Of course they were. I see the dishwasher in front of me. James cuts the tart and serves it. Jenna takes a bite and moans, "Oh, James."

He tries it and smiles. "Not bad."

They wait for me.

I won't let the fork touch my mouth. Tart

touched fork, and both tart and fork touched plate, but still . . . this feels safer. Using my tongue, I nudge the bite off the prongs without making contact with metal. Fortunately neither Jenna nor James thinks my eating technique is the least bit strange, or else they're polite. I've never had a cheese tart. It's pretty tasty even consumed this tricky way. "Fantastic," I tell James, and he points out how the salad complements it, especially the sweetness of the pears.

"The air rippled," I say.

"What air?" says Jenna.

"In the puzzle. I call it the GWW, the Great Woolly White. Didn't I mention that?" I'm getting mixed up about what I said and what I didn't. "Sometimes it looked misty like steam and sometimes thick like fog, but there was no wind, and the steam rising out of that missing section of puzzle—"

"What missing section?"

"What I thought was a crater wasn't hot or cold. In the boat it was far away, so it appeared solid; in the garden it was at my feet. Maybe it isn't air."

"It has to be air," says Jenna, "or you'd die."

"Maybe it's not weather," says James. "Can there be air without weather?"

No one knows the answer to that.

"I think it's void. Where the puzzle doesn't exist, nothing exists but the GWW. I haven't done the blues."

"They're the hardest," says Jenna.

"Sky and water," I tell James.

We can't go anywhere because I might be spotted, so we hang out, listening to Julio Iglesias, an oily singer James loves. "I want to hold you close under the rain." I imagine Julio slinking around the stage, gyrating his sexy torso, flexing his muscled arms sun-blotched pink . . . oops, not Julio's. Scratch that fantasy. It got out of hand. I settle in sideways, lopping my legs over the arms of a cushy chair. I face away from Jenna and James snuggling on the couch, but every now and then I hear noises that might be kisses. As I laze about, stuffed and tired, for once my heart doesn't ache (although other body parts do).

"When you were in the garden, could you see the other sections of the puzzle you'd put together?" Jenna asks. "The way you saw the house from the boat?"

"No."

"I wonder why."

"Maybe because the restaurant and the garden were halfway up a mountain. The house or boat wouldn't be visible from there, but if I were in the boat, then I could see the house because it's on the cove. Does that makes sense?"

"I guess."

"What were you looking for at your dad's?" says James.

"The restaurant had a mural of grape vines. The mural was like from a kid's coloring book, black outlines colored in. When I saw it, bells went off. Where have I seen this? Then the busboy laid down a placemat, a white scalloped paper placemat like the one on Dad's wall, the one with the watercolor grapes. Those grapes—mushy, vague—"

"I thought they were balloons," says Jenna.

"—are completely different from the grapes on the wall, but the same. I realized it this morning. I swear that the person who painted the watercolor was in the restaurant and maybe even painted it on one of their placemats. Now the placemat is missing. What does it mean?"

Only Julio has something to say. "Here in a world of lies, you are the true."

"I'd like to see the puzzle," says James.

"Would you show it to him?" asks Jenna.

"Sure. *Uscita.* U-S-C-I-T-A. That word was everywhere. It's either the name of the café or the family's name, or it has some other Irish meaning like 'bathroom.' Oh, and this woman kept saying, *'Troppo salato.'*"

"Too much salt," says James.

"Honey, it wasn't too salty. The tart was perfect. He's such a perfectionist," Jenna scolds and brags simultaneously.

"Not the tart," says James. "*Troppo salato* means too much salt. In Italian."

"That's impossible."

"So they were speaking Italian?" says Jenna.

"No, it's Ireland. They were speaking Irish."

"*Troppo salato* means too much salt in Italian," James insists.

I swing around to look at them lying there all tangled up. "Maybe it's Irish too."

"No way," says James.

"No way?"

"Maybe it is, James," says Jenna.

"Spell *uscita* again."

"U-S-C-I-T-A."

"I'll look it up on the web." He disappears down the hall, and while we wait, Jenna straightens her clothes and pushes her hair around. "*Uscita* means 'exit' in Italian," he shouts.

"I guess that settles it." Jenna applies some gloss.

"Whose side are you on?" I ask her.

"Side?" Jenna's face contorts in misery while I rant about what a know-it-all James is because he's a C-H-E-F, forcefully but quietly so James can't hear.

He returns, oblivious, "If it's Ireland, why were the signs in Italian? You're all mixed up."

I jump up. "You know what? I'm going home. Thanks for lunch."

Jenna and James chase after me, with Jenna begging, "You can't walk home—we have to drive you, Frannie, please."

We ride down the elevator in James's apartment building in silence. I push ONE instead of LOBBY so the trip feels endless. We have to wait while the door opens, we look out, realize it's the wrong floor, the doors close again, and James hits the button labeled L. "Why are you sure it's Ireland?" he says when we hit the lobby.

"Because my dad and I are from there. Way back when. Because the box has Celtic knots carved in."

I bang through the doors and hope they slam on him as I hear him say, "What does that have to do with the price of olives?"

"Olives? What do olives have to do with anything?" My arms fly out like bat wings as I rage across the parking lot.

"What's your problem?" he shouts.

I whirl around. "I know my dad. Why would he give me a puzzle of Italy? He wouldn't."

"It's Ireland," says Jenna. "I'm sure you're right, Frannie."

"Maybe you don't know your dad," says James.

"I know my dad!"

"It's true, James. Frannie and her dad were really, really close."

I want to scream. There's nothing about Dad that I don't know. I get his brain. The sun is beating down, and the heat off the pavement fries my feet right through my rubber soles. "I forgot sunblock," Jenna whines. She's obsessed with her lily-white skin because she burns to a crisp in no time flat.

James speaks reasonably, as reasonably as to a five-year-old. "All I'm saying is, why was that sign in Italian and why was everyone speaking Italian?"

"Everyone wasn't, only that lady."

"Are you sure? You know, the next time you go into the puzzle, you should take an Italian-English dictionary."

"Shut up, okay?" We're next to the car straddling two spaces and the discarded pizza box. I bet the people in the car had a huge fight and were too angry to park properly. They more abandoned the car than parked it. I bet they were coming home to stuff themselves with pizza, and the car got abandoned rather than parked and no one was hungry anymore. In fact everyone had a stomachache without consuming a single slice. A really big stomachache, the way I do right now.

James picks up the box and throws it in a trash can. Am I supposed to think he's a good person as a result?

As I get in the car, I hear him whisper, "Why is she so angry?"

"Shussh," says Jenna.

Why *am* I so angry?

24

"We'll do it up there."

I follow the direction of her finger to the hayloft, a platform of crisscrossed planks with tufts of straw poking through here and there. Seen from where we're standing, the loft floor, which extends halfway across the barn, is our ceiling. I imagine, between those old slats, a foot trapped. A little girl skips across, her foot plunges through. Stuck forever: a little girl's foot in a white ankle sock and a black patent leather shoe. Wouldn't it be surreal to have a whole ceiling studded with little girls' feet?

"Are you listening, Frances?"

Harriet has taken to calling me Frances. I suppose she thinks of it as a form of discipline.

"Of course I'm listening."

"We'll launch the parachutes from that window," she says. The loft window has no glass, only several boards hammered over it. It's huge.

"Looks dangerous."

"It's not dangerous."

Rickety floor, giant loft window. Is it only the illusion of dangerous? Oh well, life is an illusion, whatever that means.

"It's all explained here, under 'Egg Drop.'" Harriet thrusts a book into my hands. She chatters on about how, for someone with my experience, it will be a breeze, she's bought all the supplies. She throws out an arm—here they are, stacked on the table: tissue paper in every color, a mountain high; giant bottles of Elmer's glue; boxes of toothpicks; paintbrushes. With that, General Honker aims herself at the barn door and strides out.

In my absence (which I managed to extend for a week, will explain later), Rocco has named his lizard Leo and built him a home, a box furnished with several rocks, twigs, and pine needles. Campers huddle around, beaming down at Leo, while Rocco spins tales. "While I fall asleep, he sings in my ear."

"He should be in a circus," says Pearl the Tiara Girl. "An itty-bitty circus with itty-bitty animals."

Lark buzzes by. "Did he tell you that Leo can fly?"

"He might have mentioned that," I say, while scouring the index for "Egg Drop."

She scoots back, shoves her face into Rocco's, and barks, "Well, he can't."

"Lark, you know what? This isn't your group." I shoo her out the door past a boy named Seymour who is tormenting the Barbie twins, Beatrice and Amber, by shouting, "Barbies have boobs."

Far off, down at the lake, kids climb into canoes. Paddles wave every which way, campers nearly beheading their boat partners as they try to follow Simon's instructions. Nature Man, knee-deep in water, wades from boat to boat, correcting each camper's grip, demonstrating how the paddle works. On the dock sits the ENP. I'm guessing she's painting her toenails because 1) when I arrived this morning, a pileup of kids was begging to carry her polish, and 2) it looks like it judging from the way she's sitting: One leg is bent so her thigh hugs her chest; her head bends down over her toes. Every so often her arm swings out to a camper standing next to her, then swings back. I assume the camper is holding out the polish so she can dip the brush in.

On the tennis court, kids take turns as a machine fires balls at them. They miss often but occasionally connect and send balls soaring. There's a moment when all heads rise, following the trajectory until the ball bounces into the foot-high weeds surrounding the decrepit court. Harriet, visiting there now, applauds each player's disaster.

As I turn back to the barn, Beatrice runs into me, throws her arms around my waist, and clings. "Don't leave us."

"Why would I leave you?"

The campers gather, shoving to be the one closest. "Hazel says you don't like it here," says Amber.

"Is that true?" Brandon asks.

"Why would you think that?"

"I didn't say that," says Hazel.

"Because she threw away the collage," says Isabel. "She" is Harriet. "It's in the big black garbage bag behind the barn."

"Because you make faces," Pearl says. Hazel whacks her on the back to shut her up, but Pearl gives no ground. "It's true, she does. Like you're bored or hate us."

Rocco offers the lizard. "You can hold Leo." He's got it gripped around the middle. Poor thing. Held in such a tight fist, Leo's diamond-shaped head with its large headlight eyes bulges out one end while the tail droops out the other.

"Loosen up. He can't breathe."

"Yes, he can," says Rocco.

"Do you want to kill him?"

Rocco sucks in his cheeks as he gives that thought. Obviously I've suggested something that isn't out of the question. "Give Leo to me."

I put out my hand, and Leo pads on. He rests there, perfectly still. Every so often his eyes blink. It seems like a conscious choice, *Now I will blink*, thick lids descend and rise. He looks wise.

"All right, everybody. Today your activity is to go outside and find something beautiful. Anything that you think is beautiful. When you come back, you have to explain why it's beautiful. Get going."

Later, outside, amidst the treasures they've collected—pinecones, leaves, rocks, wildflowers— all spread across the top of the picnic table, I settle down to read about the Egg Drop. The Barbies have attached themselves; I wear one on each side. Kneeling on the bench with their dolls beside them, they hunch over the book. I scan the instructions and provide them with the gist. "To make para-chutes, we thin the glue with water, cut the tissue into shapes—"

"What kind of shapes?"

"A flower?"

"It could be a giant flower or a butterfly, what-ever you want. Then you paint every inch of the tis-sue with glue."

"Check it out and kiss it." Seymour grabs Beatrice's Barbie and grinds her face into the book. Beatrice pummels him.

"That's enough, Seymour, get lost." I straighten Barbie's prom dress, fluff the ruffles, smooth her hair, and return her to Beatrice. "When the tissue dries, it's stiff, so when someone drops the para-chute from the hayloft, it holds its shape and catches the wind. It should float down."

A meaty arm sweeps across the table, wiping it clean. "A lot of debris here," says Simon. He swings a leg over the bench to straddle it and sets his butt down. He upends a paper bag. What looks like a hero sandwich wrapped in foil falls out.

"What are you doing?"

Simon looks down at himself as if he expects to discover it. "What?"

Figure it out, I'm not telling you.

"Is this seat taken or something?" he inquires after a minute.

"That is not debris. I sent the Eagles to find beautiful objects. Art in nature."

"Those leaves?"

"And rocks and pinecones and flowers."

"We don't care," says Amber.

"I thought you were the nature counselor—don't you know anything? Are you such a clod that you can't see the beauty and uniqueness in a leaf?" I scramble around, picking up things, although it's hard to tell the difference between what's been lying on the ground and what was knocked off the table. Nevertheless I smooth the leaves and arrange the pinecones as if they are on display and have good and bad sides. Simon sits there and chews.

Oil from the hero drips down the side of his hand and his large tongue laps it.

"Want some?" He holds out half the sandwich.

I shake my head and give him my most withering glare. He picks up a leaf and takes a bite. A hearty bite. The Barbies squeal.

Simon chews, swallows, and takes a swig of water to wash it down. "I eat art," he says.

I don't know what to say, I really don't. Is art a joke? Is everything a joke? I bet he would plug in his iPod and veg on raucous music right in the middle of the Egyptian Temple of Dendur, even though it's the most spiritual place on the planet. Dad and I would sit silently for an hour in the majestic glass room that the Metropolitan Museum built to house it. "I bet you've never heard of the Temple of Dendur."

"You win." He takes another bite of leaf and chews slowly.

As the Barbies holler to everyone in the vicinity that Simon eats art, he finds a napkin in his paper sack. He has white spots. On his left cheek. I notice them just before the napkin swipes it clean.

"Mold." The word pops out.

"Mold?"

"On your face. There were little white fuzzies."

I've injured him. I know instantly because he breaks out in a swaggering smile. Yep, wide cocky grin, but the eyes hurt. Just like Mona scoop-necked Lisa. Just like Dad said. The eyes are the key.

Simon stands up. He stuffs the remainder of his sandwich and the crumpled napkin back in the bag. He's broken out in red blotches that are not from the sun. "Funny," he says.

He's accusing *me* of funny? *He's* the jokester.

"But there were these spots. Oh, it was probably that white sunblock you use."

"Nope, shaving cream. I probably didn't wipe my face after I shaved this morning." He takes off toward the lake. The ENP stops him. Laying her hand on his arm, she ogles adoringly, tilting her head much farther back than necessary (if you ask me) to make him feel taller. He accompanies her to the cabin porch, hoists a large carton onto his shoulder, and, like a sherpa in Nepal, follows her.

So big mystery solved. No mold. Shaving cream. On Dad's face. It must have congealed while he lay there.

Barbie One pulls my sleeve. "What about the egg?"

"After you make the parachute, you glue toothpicks together to make a basket. Paper it with tissue and glue the basket to the parachute."

I remember, one leg forward, one back, Dad folded over, limp as tissue. "Then you glue the basket to the parachute, and put an egg in the basket. A raw egg. When you drop the parachute, you hope the egg doesn't break."

"Will it?" asks Beatrice.

"Probably."

25

Mom hands me a hammer. "Smash the ends, honey."

In case you don't know—why would you?—when planning to use a tree branch in a flower arrangement, splinter the ends. It can drink water more easily.

While I do this, Mom untangles the branches from one another, carefully so the twiggy offshoots don't break and the red berries don't fall off. It takes patience and is remarkably tedious, which I point out, and to which she predictably replies, "They cost money." Money is a major motivator with Mom—that is, saving money. She considers it a holy virtue, even though she is not religious. If she were, "Thou shalt save" would be right at the top of her own personal ten commandments.

Mom's hair is falling into her face. She keeps blowing upward to get willful strands out of her sight line as she expertly twists wire around the branches, creating a wedding spray to decorate an arbor, the sacred place a bride and groom will marry (so they can get divorced five years later). Working since early morning, she's completed dozens of identical centerpieces and a few gigantic flower fantasies as tall as I am. She's up to her ankles in leaves and cuttings.

Suppose this is my last day on earth and I don't know it?

I've been thinking about that for days, ever since I solved the mold mystery. Dad waking up, making coffee, walking into the bathroom, lathering up, dying. Wake, brew, walk, lather, die.

Mom wipes her hands on her apron. "Just a few more branches, Frannie." She guides Andy and Carmen as they manipulate a particularly large creation out the door and into the truck. "Be sure to tell the Wilsons that the berries are poison," Mom says. "We don't want to kill Emmett." Emmett is their cat.

I break off a berry and put it on my tongue. It sits there.

Meanwhile I read the small print on the insecticide spray: *Kills 16 different kinds of bugs, including slugs and caterpillars, but is safe to use on fruits and vegetables.* I wonder if I should give up fruits and vegetables. I like lettuce.

Does it seem odd that, on the one hand, I'm so worried that I'm going to die that I read the small print on plant spray while, on the other hand, I coddle a poison berry on my tongue? Does it seem like a petite contradiction: to be thinking of killing myself and afraid of dying simultaneously? What is that? *What is that?*

Maybe if I'm dead, I won't be afraid I'm going to die. It would be such a relief not to worry so much.

Mom walks back in. "I heard about the poison collage."

I tuck the berry into my cheek. "That's over, we're doing parachutes."

She stiffens. "Parachutes. You can't drop those campers in parachutes, what from trees? That's, that's—" She's having an attack of the sputters.

"You can't build parachutes, do you understand? That's completely dangerous. That's insane, that's what it is, insane. Does Harriet know? Oh, God, she's going to call me. What was that poison thing anyway? What in the world were you thinking?"

"Art. It's called art."

"That's something—"

"What?"

I'm waiting for her to say it—that's something your dad would do—but she doesn't. She throws up her hands in despair. "Why are you doing this?"

The implication is "to me." Why are you doing this to me?

"Mom, they're tissue-paper parachutes. You put an egg in them. They don't carry people, they carry eggs."

"Oh."

"Harriet's idea."

"Oh." She smiles sheepishly. She picks up some wire, fiddles around, spinning it between her fingers. "I'm glad to hear that, Frannie. How's that boy?"

I can't answer because there's a berry on my tongue.

She leans down to whisk up debris under the table, dumping it into an already bulging garbage bag. I take the berry out of my mouth.

Mom grabs my hand. "What's that? A berry. You put a berry in your mouth?"

"Just testing."

"Testing? Testing what? That doesn't make sense. Don't do that." Mom smacks her hand into her forehead. Her face is flushed. "Do you know how much you mean to me? Do you, Frannie?"

God, she overreacts to everything.

"What would I do if—"

I distract her by clamping the stem of a rose between my teeth. I'm a Spanish dancer. I wag my head so the rose flops up and down.

"I'm serious, Frannie."

I keep wagging.

Her shoulders slump, her arms hang by her sides. I remove the rose. "Are you tired?"

She shakes her head.

"Are you all right?"

She goes to her mini fridge for a bottle of water. She presses the bottle to her forehead and to each cheek before unscrewing the top and gulping some. I take the hammer and splinter another branch. Maybe she'll follow my example and get back to work. Come on, Mom, do what I do. "So how is that nice boy?" she asks again. "The one at camp."

"I never said he was nice."

"Are you sure? I thought—"

"He ate a leaf."

She smiles. "Why?"

"Because he's a Neanderthal."

"Maybe he likes you."

Maybe he likes me? Is she talking to a baby? Maybe he likes you, honey, that's why he threw a rock at you. I change the subject. "Was Dad ever in Italy, Mom?"

She plays with her bottle of water, swinging it back and forth. She takes another swig. Her cheeks inflate. She's buying time. Finally she swallows. I study her face. Scrutinize it. Hmm, a hint of amusement. Gear up, here comes a frenemy moment—she'll say something super-innocuous about Dad, a futile attempt to conceal her conde- scension from me, truth finder.

"So was he in Italy?"

"He was, he absolutely was." She grins.

"What's funny about it?"

"What made you ask?"

"I don't know."

She cracks up. She's tickled to death at the thought of Dad in Italy, and when she's finished chuckling, she ruffles my hair to the extent that hedge hair can be ruffled. Her face softens as if she's ooing and aahing over a kitten, as if I'm Emmett.

"What's so funny?"

"Nothing. What made you ask, sweetie?"

"No reason, absolutely none."

"I don't believe you."

"Tough."

Mom takes a step back. "Don't be rude."

"I hate this place."

"My shop?" Mom looks around.

I rip my hand down a branch, spraying off twigs and berries. "I hate where I am." I spit out the words. I spit them right at her.

Mom looks at the naked branch, and the berries rolling around. She's going to start screaming about what a nightmare I am, about the waste of money and how hard she works and something about the stupid wedding. But she doesn't. She puts out her arms. "Come here."

"No."

"Frannie."

"I don't want you." Why doesn't she get that? I back out of the workroom and make it out the door in time to flag down the truck as it leaves the lot.

26

Andy gives in to my plea to make a quick stop at the bookstore before he drops me off, and he forces me to listen to country music, which turns out to be a mind-calmer. When I walk into the house, I hear the vacuum. Rosanna must be here. It's not her usual day.

I make my leisurely way up the stairs leafing through my new English-Italian phrase book. Although it's impossible that Mr. Super Chef might be right—not Ireland, Italy—I bought a book, just in case.

Good grief, she's vacuuming my room.

The board has been spun from under the bed over to the window. Piles of sorted pieces stacked around the edge of the puzzle have toppled, perhaps from a quick swivel or the force of Rosanna's yank. Jigsaw pieces are far flung, like shattered glass.

"Stop!" I shout. It's one of her English words. *Por favor*, I also shout, which everyone knows means "please," but Rosanna, oblivious, on her knees, is ramming the vacuum nozzle into every nook and cranny under the bed. I hit the OFF switch.

The silence takes a second to register; then Rosanna sits back on her heels. "Frannita." She hops up and begins scolding me in a torrent of Spanish. I get the message but not the words, except possibly "dirty" and *mucho*. She's talking about my room. "Surprise," I tell her, "*Sorpresa. Sorpresa* for Mom." I gesture toward the puzzle. *Puzzle* is not a word I know in Spanish, I've only studied for two years. I close the bedroom door and put my finger to my lips. This is hush-hush. Secret.

Secreto. Mom does not know. Mel does not know. I tell her that in Spanish. Thank God he hasn't wandered in. Thank God on summer Saturdays he shops at the farmers' market. Right this second he's probably feeling up corn. He claims that when you buy corn on the cob, you can tell if the kernels are small and plump by squeezing the husks. Isn't that fascinating?

In case you're wondering why Rosanna hasn't vacuumed in here since I brought the puzzle home weeks ago, I told her not to. I announced it in front of Mom, who nodded approval. Nodded vigorously—Mom doesn't speak much Spanish, and even when she can say something, she indicates instead, or overindicates, to make the point. Because Mom believes it's character building for teenagers to clean their own rooms, I was able to keep Rosanna away from the puzzle and my beautiful carved box.

The box. Where is it?

"Box," I say to her. Do I know that word in Spanish? I can't remember. Rosanna waits. It's hopeless. I flatten to look under the bed. Not there.

"Box?" Rosanna shakes her head. I speed-hunt through the room, flinging up sheets she stripped off the bed, pillows, dirty clothes. Oh, there it is. In a safe place, cushioned by Dad's shirts, it's nestled in one of the open cardboard boxes. Box, I show her what I was referring to. *Secreto muy grande.*

Rosanna beams and says something that I don't understand.

"Uscita." I toss it up and see if it lands.

"Who?" she replies in English.

So *uscita* is not Spanish. In fact, I'll look it up right now. There it is, in my Italian phrase book, under "Signs & Public Notices": Exit: *uscita.*

For sure, the puzzle is Italy. Dad has been in Italy, in this ancient town, whatever it is. And mom thinks that's funny. Obviously *he* didn't think it was funny, or he wouldn't have made me this puzzle.

In an attempt to hustle Rosanna out of the room, I collect her dust towel and cleaning sprays (poison for sure). She swipes her finger across my bureau.

Dust, she shows me. She moves some big boxes, revealing crumbs from old sandwiches, crushed peanuts. She points out an empty cellophane bag (red licorice) and a shriveled plum under the bureau.

"I'll vacuum," I say. *Yo* vacuum. Please, Rosanna. I give her a big hug. I hear Mel pull into the driveway as I maneuver Rosanna out the door.

After flipping my Italian phrase book onto the bed, I hit the ON switch. While the vacuum roars, a decoy, I get on hands and knees and hunt for jigsaw pieces, combing the shag one small area at a time. Suppose a piece got sucked up in the vacuum? I can't think about that. I don't even want to consider it. Good grief, here's one on the bathroom floor.

I'd better check out the vacuum bag: hold it over the trash basket and rip. This is disgusting. It's packed with dust balls and food bits, but fortunately, no puzzle parts.

I must make a decision about going back in.

Control. I have no control. But . . . but, but, I have noticed that my going into the puzzle happens late at night after hours of puzzle work, a consequence of dizziness and near-hypnotic concentration.

I don't want to go back in until I'm absolutely ready.

So I've given up working nights. That's why I stayed home from camp for an entire week. "Toodle-oo," I told Mel every morning and pranced out the door. "Tooth infection," I fibbed to Mr. DeAngelo. The bus rumbled on, and I sped behind the garage and waited, giving Beastoid time to retreat to his study. After about a half hour, I snuck back in through the kitchen door.

It was risky. Mel can get sidetracked by the most boring things. Once Mom saw this book about coal. *The History of Coal.* She bought it for him, and you know what he said? "I've already read that." No kidding. There is always the possibility that he'll get obsessed with something in the newspaper, something endless and dreary like an article about peach pits, and put off serfs until later. "Oh, I couldn't put the paper down, freestone peaches are so riveting."

But mainly he's reliable. "I could set my watch by that man." I once watched a TV show about an old man who did everything the same way every single day, and when he got murdered, that's what his landlady said. "I could set my watch by that man."

Hide in plain sight. Ever heard that expression? I wasn't in plain sight, but my bedroom was hardly deep cover either. Knowing there was no reason for Mel to enter my room (and that he did not venture out of his study until six), I worked days undetected for a week. Kept myself alert at all times, too. If I got loopy or droopy—so close to the puzzle that I could lick it—I took a break.

I never fell in.

Here's a puzzle piece on the shelf. Boy, Rosanna creates a mighty wind. It landed right next to Dad's unfinished sculpture, my precious wavy bird. Perhaps the bird was guarding it, keeping it safe.

I place the jigsaw piece on my palm and blow off specks of dirt. It's plain, yellow with white letters:

via. No other piece has had letters on it. I wonder where it goes.

I cruise the empty spots. The hulk of the church is gray, but the dome glows a bright lemon. No match for the muddy yellow in my v-i-a piece. Along the cove, buildings in different shades of rose and maroon have yellow stripes, but all as pale as tapioca. Jumping to the other side of the puzzle, I work my way down from the top: the restaurant, garden, stone steps, rooftops. Is there a dot of mustard by that building? The faintest smudge? I don't hear the satisfying click because the vacuum is blasting, but the puzzle surface is smooth, inter-locking curves in perfect harmony. I love it when I make a match.

I celebrate by turning off the vacuum.

Break time. Study Italian time. James was right. Chef Man tells the truth. Hard for third wheel to accept. Puzzle must be Italy. I try to get into Dad's head about this. Why would Dad give me Italy? He didn't like opera. He loved pizza. Did he tell me about Italy? Was it a bedtime story? Did I forget?

I know my dad. Don't I?

I'd better keep this phrase book with me at all times in case I fall into the puzzle by accident. Since it's the size of a chocolate bar, it will slip easily into my pocket.

When I pick up the book and roll onto the bed, something stabs my back. Another missing piece. More letters, and, like the other, mustard yellow with white lettering: GRAVINO. I fall off the bed and, in a second, make the match: VIA GRAVINO. A place? A street?

I hope that is truly the last of the missing pieces.

Suppose my 1000-piece puzzle is now a 999-piece puzzle? Worse, a 989-piece puzzle? The way to my father, if this is the way, could be blocked.

Don't think about that.

Study.

Prepare.

I prop up my pillows, sock them a few times, sit back and wiggle to get truly comfortable, then thumb through the book. Father. *Padre.* "Is there a campsite nearby?" *C'è un camping qui vicino?* Camping? I hate camping. I hope I don't need to camp. "Can I buy ice?" *Si può comprare del ghiaccio? Ghiaccio?* How do you pronounce that word? I'm passing on ice. *Dov'è?* Where is? *Dov'è mio padre?* Where is my father?

27

The sky is dumping rain.

An enormous yellow slicker and black rubber boots splash into the barn. Slung over its shoulder, a bulging plastic garbage bag clangs when it's swung down and hits the floor. An arm flies up and knocks back the hood, and out springs the screaming red hair. The Honker's face is wet. From the bottom of her somewhat pointed chin, water drips like a leaky faucet. She hunts around in a big patch pocket, produces a red kerchief that she rubs over her face.

In strolls Simon, sopping wet in a T-shirt and

cargo shorts. He stops, shakes his head, spraying water in every direction, and wrings out his shirt by twisting the front. Crowding in behind is a group of campers. He herds them over to a corner where they shed their rain gear. Not that I'm paying attention. I'm too busy and too miserable. The hot, sticky air reminds me of a sauna Jenna and I once took because she insisted it was good for the skin. I flap Dad's shirt for air-conditioning while I supervise parachute construction. Except for Simon's little corner, where he settles his campers in a circle, I've taken over the barn. My kids, on the floor, wield scissors, dip brushes in vats of glue, and bathe volumes of tissue paper with it. I'm counting the hours until I can get back to the puzzle.

This morning I wondered if I had made a mistake. A colossal mistake. Suppose by working sensibly, keeping alert at all times, I blew my chance to enter the puzzle again? Suppose I blew my chance to see Dad? I have no control. Why do I think I have control?

"I don't know what kind to make, Frannie. What kind of parachute should I make?" Pearl trails me, tugging on my shirt, driving me nuts.

"I'm sure you can figure it out. You'd better get started—everyone else has been working for a week." Harriet nods approvingly. I can't help overhearing Simon's booming voice. "Sensitivity, dudes, let's hear it for sensitivity." He insists that they cheer several times until he's satisfied with the level of pep. "Today we're working on friendship and conversation," he tells them. Mr. Marry-Me-and-Be-My-Canoe is teaching the art of conversation.

A crackle of lightning, and everyone stops what they're doing, waiting for the boom of thunder to follow. "Will the roof fall?" asks Isabel.

"Maybe."

"The roof won't fall," says Harriet. "That's ridiculous. What are you talking about, Frances?" Digging into the garbage bag, she produces several pots that she proceeds to place strategically to catch the many leaks. Meanwhile, the rain on the roof sounds like animals stampeding, and the damp, seeping through the old boards, creates areas of discoloration like sweat marks. Sure, the roof won't fall, but the barn is sweating. Like that's normal. The sides will collapse, I'll be buried under debris for days and end up a vegetable. If I ever see the puzzle again, I won't even recognize it.

"Look, Barbie's swimming pool." Seymour grabs Beatrice's doll and dunks her head in a pot. Fortunately, the pot has barely an inch of water. Beatrice snatches the doll back, and to my surprise Amber starts whacking Seymour with her Barbie, landing blows all over his head and shoulders. He stumbles backward and almost falls on Lark's parachute. Lark throws her body over it as if she's protecting her baby from gunfire.

I yank Seymour away, but Amber, the tiger, keeps swinging. Simon lifts her into the air. "Sensitivity, both of you." He moves two campers over to make space, drops Amber into the circle, and pushes Seymour in next to her. Seymour has not been working on a parachute. His sole interests are tormenting girls and gum chewing. He takes wads he's done with and sticks them on himself. Simon plucks one from Seymour's forehead and flicks it into the garbage can.

"I don't know what to make," whines Pearl. "Frannie, what should I make?"

"I don't know."

Lark's parachute, decorated with the face of a lion, is a remarkable creation. She's slathered glue onto several identically sized circles of yellow tissue, about three feet in diameter, and stuck them together so the main body of the parachute has a little extra weight and stiffness. I use it for a demonstration model. The parachutes are most likely to waft down gently and the eggs to land safely if the main frame is shaped as Lark's is, I show them. She acknowledges my compliment with a wiggle of her shoulders and a few thrusts of her fists. On top of the parachute she's built the lion's face: a wreath of short strips of brown, gold, and copper for a shaggy mane, flat round black eyes, a cone of brown tissue for the nose, and an open gaping mouth—the better to eat you with—which she's working on now. As she concentrates on shaping a twisted rope of tissue into an oval and gluing it down, her own mouth gapes open in imitation. "I'm going to stuff red tissue inside," she says.

"The tongue?"

"The tongue." She sticks hers out. "I'll rest the egg on it."

"I hope mine drops like a bomb," says Gregor, who is gluing tissue around an inflated balloon (another technique suggested by the book). When the tissue dries, he'll pop the balloon with a pin, and the hardened tissue should remain balloon shaped. Then he must cut a small hole in the tissue balloon and glue in a bunch of tissue shreds or a toothpick basket to carry the egg. Before Amber got hijacked into sensitivity training, the Barbies were building a boat parachute, powder blue with silver stars.

"Suppose the wind won't carry it? Suppose there's no wind?" asks Beatrice.

"If there's no wind, the ground will be splattered with yolks and broken parachutes." Out of the corner of my eye I see that Simon has arranged his campers in pairs. They face each other cross-legged.

"I don't know what to make," says Pearl.

"A butterfly. Sit right down here and make a butterfly." Before I scream, but I don't say that.

"What color?"

"Pink."

Rocco is making a centipede parachute. Many legs, different-colored strips of tissue, dangle off a long rectangle, the main body. His bug could never walk because all the legs are different sizes. He doesn't cut tissue, he rips it. He and his sister are from different worlds—she methodical and exacting, he charismatically chaotic. Sitting on his shoulder, watching him splatter as much glue on himself as on the tissue, is Leo. Isabel has tied a red ribbon around his rubbery green tail, and he looks festive, a Christmas lizard in August.

"Leo can fly. Who wants to hold Leo?" asks Rocco. "For five dollars, anyone can hold him who wants to."

"Me, and I'm not paying." I place an open hand next to Rocco's shoulder, and Leo pads on. I contemplate him, he contemplates me. I think he's smiling, like a Buddha, as if he has wisdom and knowledge that all of us don't. He seems peaceful. Leo the anxiety-free lizard. Brave to be anxiety-free when your primary caregiver is a maniac. Every so often his throat contracts and inflates again. Every so often his tongue flicks out, but otherwise he remains still. Have you ever heard the expression "No one's home," meaning that the person is vacant, empty, even soulless? With Leo, someone is definitely home. Could he be Dad reincarnated? I know that's a bizarre notion, but imagine: Your dad dies and you find a lizard, keep it in a box, and, unbeknownst to you, it's really your dad. You figure that out because one night he crawls into the moo shu pork, your dad's favorite Chinese food. I could draw that—a perfect white box and Leo's triangular head and sweet bulging eyes peeking over the top. I could call the drawing "Dad's Back."

Dad is back and waiting for me in the puzzle.

Suppose I can't get in again?

That thought is tormenting me.

I put Leo in his box on top of a pile of dry grass. I tickle his tail. He stretches his legs before moving away.

"I'll do it with Frannie. We'll demonstrate," I hear Simon announce.

I whip around.

He waves me over to his little circle.

"That's okay, thanks anyway, we're busy over here."

"Frances, Simon needs your help," Honker rasps in my ear.

"Well, that's too bad, I'm very busy. Keep working," I tell the kids, but they don't. While Simon keeps waving and calling, "Come on, Frannie," they look at Simon, then at me. Back and forth. Their brushes, poised in the air, drip glue; scissors pause mid slice.

"Frannie, Frannie, Frannie," Simon chants and they all join in.

The Honker gives me a push, the nerve. While everyone cheers, I step over and around children and parachutes. It seems a very long distance to Simon and not long enough. "What am I supposed to do?" I inquire in a most businesslike way, and in response, he sits down on the floor and crosses his legs. I follow suit, facing him. He inches closer until our knees are touching, and without being obvious I avoid eye contact. My eyes dart over his shoulder, at his left ear, at the scrunched-up section of his T-shirt, the light hair on his wet arms. "We are going to close our eyes and feel each other's faces," he says.

A sudden cold sweat with the humidity at ninety. I am experiencing panic. "What does this have to do with sensitivity?"

"She'll see," he tells the campers. "Okay, dudes, are you ready?"

The dudes are ready. Even Lark is fascinated. While cradling the red tissue tongue in her hands, she stares; her eyes pop to the widest shutter opening; her thin half-moon brows rise. Rocco, riveted as well, has his finger up his nose. Hazel, engrossed in peeling glue off the tips of her fingers, stops scraping. Isabel, with a beatific grin, expects to see something romantic, while Harriet, her face all pinched and practical, is viewing the proceedings scientifically. I recognize the look from biology class, whack, down comes the chopper. "Let's slice up this frog's head, the brains are green, can everyone see this? Hey you, Jack, in the back row, can you see these brains?" She's Jack in the back row, craning to see the results of the experiment. They are all waiting. Someone has waved a magic wand, and they are statues and will be freed only by my submitting to Simon.

"We're going to shut our eyes and feel each

other's faces," Simon repeats.

I am so intent on cool, so intent. I'm going to feel his face but I'm not going to feel his face when I feel his face because someone else is sitting here knocking knees with Sensitivity Man, not Frances Anne Cavanaugh. An impersonator, a stand-in. "You're witnesses," I tell the kids. "If he doesn't shut his eyes, too, I expect you all to yell." To him I hiss, "This has nothing to do with sensitivity."

He ignores me. "On three we start. One . . . two . . . three."

I shut my eyes. You know what that's like in day-light: You're looking at the insides of your eyelids, murky shadows, and along the bottoms, a rim of lifeless light as if the sun is setting on a brown day.

After a few agonizing seconds, I feel his fingers touch my cheek, a hand presses down, skin rough and callused clumsily pats over my nose to the other cheek as if he's trying to determine my species, girl or elephant. I start to giggle. "Sorry." Get a grip, Frannie. I stick out both arms, hands up and wide open, trying to make this as silly as possible, but it's unnerving not knowing the distance or location. Whoa, my hands collide with a land mass, his face. Tap-dancing my fingers around, I climb the little mountain of his nose, encounter an eye. His lashes tickle the tip of my third finger. Intentionally I brush the wrong way across his eyebrows. I locate a blister somewhere—it's harder to identify face geography than I expect—but if I concentrate on touching him, I'm less aware of his hands touching me. What's this? His chin bone? I'm tracing the line, chin to ear, when he smoothes my lip with his finger and electricity shoots down my spine.

"That's enough." I open my eyes and am looking directly into his. Not the least bit unnerving, locking eyes with Simon is actually pleasant. I could walk right in and sit right down, stretch out across those pale blues and pitch a tent there without thinking twice. He's nice. That thought surfaces the way an object floats to the surface of water and reveals itself.

"Now Frannie has to ask me a question." He gazes steadily at me but addresses the kids.

"How did you learn to canoe?" I say. How lame is that? Utterly. And yet, do I care?

I'm not wise, but I am aware, as if another part of me is watching, that my defenses are scrambling to get back into service. I have no interest in them, because I like it where I am, paddling around in Simon's eyes, doing the breaststroke, the back-stroke, kicking from one end of the pool to the other.

"Canoe?" says Simon. "Well, my dad. My dad taught me. My folks have a cabin in the Adiron-dacks. We go there on holidays and weekends. I learned everything about the outdoors from my dad. Next year my dad and I are going to Yosemite."

Next year his dad and he . . . they've got plans.

Things they're going to do together.

"Now Frannie has to ask a follow-up question." Again he addresses the campers without breaking eye contact with me.

Next year his dad and he . . . I feel my chest cave, and other parts reflexively tighten, my arms, my neck, even my jaw stiffens trying to keep the sadness at bay. The only comfort is Simon's blue eyes. They seem to see deep inside me, right to the wound. "You know what, Frannie doesn't have to ask a question." He takes me off the hook. "I'll ask her one. What's in your pocket?"

"What?"

"Your shirt pocket. What's in it?"

"Nothing."

I slip my hand inside to prove it and find an object instantly familiar—the weight, the flatness, the jigsawed edges. What is a puzzle piece doing in my pocket? How did it get there?

I show it to him. "My dad made me a jigsaw puzzle."

Except for Jenna and James, he's the first person I've told, and it escapes me that it's not a confidence, that dozens of kids watching are also privy to this fact that has no meaning to them but means everything to me.

The spell—if this eye captivity is a spell—breaks because I glance at the puzzle piece. It's the very same one I put into the puzzle the night before. The yellow one with white printing, GRAVINO. In my mind's eye I see my hand moving over the puzzle, turning the piece so the sides line up properly, and then pressing down, feeling the click that confirms the match. Is it there and here at the same time? Or just here? And how? Why?

"Can I carry your purse? Please, please, please." I hear Pearl's unmistakable whine.

My purse? I look up. Every single person, including Simon, has turned toward the door. Behold the ENP, wearing a see-through plastic raincoat. Looking at her is like looking through a shower curtain. Even though, underneath, she's dressed in shorts and a tank top, the effect is that she isn't wearing a single thing. Every camper is dumbstruck except Pearl, clamoring to be lackey for the day. Simon stares. He licks his lips. I guess this is the real sensitivity training.

I tuck the puzzle piece back in my shirt pocket and, for safety, fasten the flap over the top.

28

I must have patted my pocket every five seconds that day, making certain the piece was still there, that it hadn't escaped or I hadn't imagined its presence—a side effect of Simon's eyes, formerly as compelling as grapefruit, revealing depth and compassion and understanding, creating confusing flutters in unexpected places. All this flesh trembling couldn't have caused a puzzle piece to transport itself through space into my shirt pocket. I mean, face pawing can electrify one's nerve endings, but induce telekinesis? I don't think so.

Arriving home, I fly from the bus into my house and up the stairs. At the bedroom door I halt and take a second to make sure I'm alone and likely to remain so. I poke my head into the stairwell leading up to the attic, Mel's hideaway office. Silence. He appears to be buried in books. I listen carefully for noises, any, anywhere. Not even a mouse. Nevertheless, opening my bedroom door softly, inch by inch, will minimize the risk of arousing Beastoid, catapulting him out of a medieval reverie into a sense of duty. "That must be dear Frannie. I'll say hello. That will shock her hair straight. Let's see, it's her hundredth return home with no greeting." I shouldn't complain about not being greeted when I crave not being greeted, not to mention that I'm borderline rude to him. Okay, not borderline. Avoiding an encounter with The Mel at all costs, I slip quietly inside my room and find Jenna, cross-legged on my bed, tears streaming rivers down her cheeks, her face crimson from crying. Around her, many balled-up white tissues create the impression that she's nesting in Styrofoam.

"James," she chokes out, and then throws herself facedown on the pillow. Her back shakes. Eventually she gets her story out (although some of it is muffled by down), about how she salted rice without tasting it first, and he said she shouldn't. You should always taste something before salting it, he told her. She tried to blot the salt off.

"You tried to get the salt off? Who are you?"

"What?"

"He tells you not to salt something and you try to rub the salt off?"

"Blot it." She flips over and grabs a bunch more tissues.

"That's ridiculous. Who are you?"

"I don't know what you mean." Her voice quivers.

"I mean it's just James everything, James this, James that. He's a food tyrant. He tells you not to salt something and you act like a serf."

"I'm not a serf."

"You're obsessed with him and you act like nothing exists but him, you don't even exist."

"That's mean, Frannie."

"Jenna, I have something important that I have to do. Excuse me." I get on my knees and slide the puzzle board out. Jenna kicks it back in.

She says, "I don't see where I'm worse than you."

"Jenna, really strange things are happening—I found this puzzle piece—" She sits up straight now. No one sits more erect than Jen. "Look." I try to be kind. "This amazing thing happened and you're carrying on about rice."

"Not rice, risotto, which is a special kind of rice." Her voice squeaks and trembles. "It takes forever to make, you have to stir it every single second, and maybe James was tired and that's why we had an awful fight." Fight, uttering the word, produces a new flood, but she swipes one eye, then the other, to stem it. "He made it with shrimp and he used the shells to flavor the broth, which was pretty ingenious, and then, you see, it needs Parmesan and that's a salty cheese. I salted it, so—" She bobs her head several times. Is she agreeing with his point of view?

"You're losing your identity."

"What's my identity?" she wails.

That is just too deep for me, I don't have time to deal with this now. Although . . . "Why am I worse than you?"

"Never mind."

"Why?"

"All you think about is the puzzle and . . ."

"And what?"

She looks around the room, eyeing the boxes that still clutter it. I can see she's trying to decide what to say, whether to say, how much to say, so I have to set her straight on the absolute obvious. "My dad and James are not the same. I mean, if you took one of those scales of justice, and put James being mean on one side and Dad being dead on the other—"

"He didn't speak to me all through dinner."

"If you put James on one side and Dad on the other, the thing would tilt totally—I can't believe I'm even explaining this to you."

"So like forever after, you hurt worse than me?"

"Maybe."

"And you get to think about yourself all the time but I don't."

"I don't think about myself all the time."

"Yes, you do. Get real. I've been so nice and you don't even notice."

"How'd you get in?"

"Huh? What?"

"Into the house, Jenna? Does Mel know you're here? I'm wondering if he's going to come barging in and see the puzzle, although he won't, will he, because you kicked it under the bed?"

Jenna gives me a long, hard look, a look she should have given James. Her eyes dry up. She smashes a tissue against her nose, honks once, balls up the tissue, and chucks it into the pile. She swings her legs off the bed and, with a sweep of her arm, knocks the tissue balls off the bed and into the wastebasket. "There, you'll never know I was here."

"Jenna, come on, I'm sure if you call James . . ." I

go into the bathroom to fix her a warm wet wash-cloth because, even though she isn't still crying, her eyes are bloodshot, and when I return barely thirty seconds later she's gone. She made less noise leaving than I did arriving, but then she's a ballet dancer and considerably more graceful than I am.

She had no right to be so sensitive. Sensitive, hmm. That word is coming up a lot today, like the day practically has a theme. There is such a huge difference between James the Albert-Waldo and— forget it. It isn't even fun to play with his name. Or nice. Maybe it was never nice. It's lonely in this house, and it is really Jenna's fault that right this second I don't even care whether telekinesis happened, and I find myself climbing the stairs to Mel's office.

I knock.

"It's open," he calls.

As I enter, he swivels from his computer to face me. His shoves his hands under his glasses and rubs his eyes; then, while they're still blinking, he presses his hands into his sides to wake up his muscles. Finally he says, "How was work?"

"Okay." I flop onto his couch. "What are you doing?"

"Me?"

Why does he always make it seem like a miracle if I ask him a question? He is the only other person in the room—who else would I be talking to? His room—I guess Mom decorated. It's got her unmistakable antiseptic touch, with aluminum-pole bookshelves that arrived in a box with directions that Mom's delivery guy, Andy, had to decipher while Mom and Mel stood there uselessly saying things like "Don't step on a pole" (they were rolling about), and "Be sure you don't lose the screws. Did you lose the screws? Where are the screws?" and spinning other variations on the screw-disaster scenario.

Mel's books, floor to ceiling, are mostly old, with faded torn cloth covers. I bet the paper inside is yellowing and brittle, and if the books could think, they would feel out of place on this metal contraption. Mel probably has the books cata-logued in some maniacally compulsive way. There are labels on the shelves too far away for me to read. Except for his PC, electric pencil sharpener, paper clip holder, and jar of identical black pens, his desk is a Plexiglas wasteland. OhmyGod, he's a reaction. He's a reaction to Dad. Poor mom, that's why she hooked up with him. He's the un-Dad. Dad with his cozy artist's studio coated with saw-dust, Dad who would have leaned back and plunked his legs up on his drafting table. Mel, on the other hand, performs some infinitesimal adjustment to his glasses, repositioning them on his ears, places his elbows on the desk, clasps his hands, and cocks his head. "Is something wrong?" he asks.

"Why would something be wrong?" I snap. I do snap. I'm out of control, I'm an attack dog. "How are the serfs?" I add lamely.

"Fine."

I wait for him to tell me something like how their favorite food is gopher, but he doesn't offer anything. All of a sudden he's a mite withdrawn. His face goes slack, as if he's barely aware of my presence. Even his eager puppy-dog eyes get a case of the remotes. Does he dislike me, why would he dislike me? Or, put another way, why would he like me? That's heavy, I'm not going there, so I drag myself up and head out again. "I'm going to take a nap, camp was exhausting, I might sleep through dinner, would you tell Mom?" I turn to reward him with a disarming smile—say cheese, Frannie—when I spy over his shoulder, on the wall next to his bookshelf, the grapes.

"Where did you get that?"

Mel turns to follow my glare. The missing watercolor, the painting from Dad's studio, is now framed, as if it's something elegant and valuable and utterly un-Dad. It floats—that's a term Dad taught me—meaning that the entire placemat, scallops and all, is glued to a backing, in this case minty green paper, and then the entire shebang framed, in this case, in wood that's painted—don't faint—a shimmery gold.

"Where'd you get that watercolor?"

"From your mom." He plucks it off the wall and admires it at close range. "I love it, I just love it."

"I just love it" is virtually a caress. How inappropriate and shocking. "Mom stole it from Dad's studio."

The look he gives me is truly puzzled and very nervy, considering he knows exactly what I'm talking about. She'll steal the wavy bird next. She's probably after all of Dad's things.

"To frame that painting is a total invasion of privacy."

"Whose privacy?"

"Forget it, forget it. I'm going to sleep, forget it," I tell him.

"Good idea," says Mel. He hangs the picture up and swivels to face his computer as if I'm already gone.

29

Back in my room, I crash on the bed and, reaching under, slide out the puzzle board. I've got the migrating piece clutched in my fist, and the minute that section of the puzzle comes into view, I detect the empty spot. The piece *is* missing. VIA is in the puzzle, GRAVINO is in my hand. Yet I know I didn't remove it.

Otherwise, the puzzle is undisturbed. I'm down to the blues. Along the mountain ridge, the church tower, the roofs and treetops, wherever the sky meets land, there's a hazy blue border, and along the puzzle's bottom, pieces of stone quay and muddy beach have a deeper blue and a greenish-blue rim where they dip into water. The little dinghy still floats all by its lonesome, waiting for me to supply the sea around it. The most daunting is yet to come, and yet the power of Dad's work is evident. In the ancient buildings crammed together and gaily painted, I can sense age, tradition, and a spirit of survival. Is there someone on that balcony? Who hung out those clothes to dry? Watered the flowers? Who is shopping and visiting, who's quarreling and laughing inside shuttered windows and on the steep and shadowy streets hidden from view? At the cove a cluster of patio umbrellas and dabs of color suggest the bustle of a seaside café in the summertime. What delicious snacks are they feasting on? I thumb through my Italian phrase book. *Torta*, cake, *fragola*, strawberries, *melone*, melon, *gelato*—that's a word I already know. One tilted umbrella, a bright tangerine, is tantalizing. Who's hidden there, shaded from the sun? Lovers secretly kissing? A smudge of red. Is that a flower, a person?

The empty spot where GRAVINO belongs will complete the town. When I put it back, will it stay there? What is the point of plugging something into the puzzle if it's going to unplug itself and relocate, say, in my shoe? Oh well. I reach down to lock GRAVINO into place once again, and as I hear that familiar click of a match, I feel a pull as if my whole body is being sucked by a giant vacuum, all hearing obliterated by a deafening whoosh. Within a second I am helpless in a swirling vortex, spun downward, traveling through a funnel of wind suspended and propelled by its fearsome force and then flipped like a flimsy guppy, head over tail, and land abruptly but softly on my back with a bit of a bounce.

On my back. On prickly ground. Eyes tightly shut.

Birds twittering. The caw of a gull, again and yet again. Recognizing a sound gives me the nerve to open my eyes. A breeze is warm and gentle; tall weedy greens rustle and sway around me, some topped with yellow and purple. I appear to be lying in a bed of leggy grass and wildflowers. Turning my head this way and that, checking agility and connections between neck and back, I notice movement in the distance. I sit up.

Hikers stride up a trail, outfitted to the max, backpacks like buildings, heavy boots laced over their ankles, each step stamped with seriousness of purpose by the stabs of their walking sticks with each upward clomp. "*Ciao*," I shout. "*Ciao.*"

I scramble up and brush and shake off the dirt as the six of them, smiling, tromp toward me. I recognize "*Buon giorno,*" which basically means hello, but nothing else they say. One of them scoops my Italian phrase book off the ground, dusts it off, and presents it to me. While they wait patiently, I skim through it. "Is there any danger of an avalanche?" That sentence is definitely useless. "Why?" "When?" "How far?" Nope. Aha. "Where can I find . . ." I attempt that phrase, speaking slowly and pointing out the words at the same time, *"Dove posso trovare Via Gravino?"*

They exchange looks. No one has a clue. "Vernazza?" one suggests, but not too confidently.

Vernazza? What's that? Another long pause while I locate the word *town*. *"La città?"*

"Sì."

Buildings, water, little boats. *"I palazzi, l'acqua, le barchette."* That takes much page flipping.

"Vernazza," they all agree.

"Dov'è Vernazza?"

They all point in the direction they came from. I am so relieved that I'll be walking down rather than up. *"Grazie,"* I repeat many times, shouting it after them in happiness as soon as I locate the word in the chapter called "Polite Phrases."

I trudge down a steep gravel path and then proceed down wide stone steps cut into rock. Even though this trek requires considerable balance and my squat-and-step routine, at least now it's a routine. I manage pretty well. I feel . . . strong. Competent. The air around me is clear and fresh, unlike in other puzzle visits, but the sky above is mottled as if too many colors have been mixed in a bottle and diluted, leaving a trace color but no discernable shade. It might be filmy gray or brown or purplish, the remains of smoke from a fire long extinguished, hanging about in the atmosphere. Behind me, up the mountain, a low building with a gray awning juts out from the cliff. It's the restaurant I visited. Ahead, Vernazza.

The town reveals itself with surprising suddenness. One second I am struggling down yet another steep step, the next I find myself on a street with narrow houses on both sides, both gayer and shabbier than they appear in the puzzle, gorgeous sun-baked colors flecking off in big patches, bow-fronted balconies dotted with friendly pots of geraniums, clotheslines crisscrossing from second floor to second floor, hung with pants and shirts that flutter like flags of welcome. One second I'm alone, the next I'm surrounded by life, a parade of school-children, two by two, all in matching white shirts and navy skirts and pants. Women stroll and shop, carrying purchases in fishnet bags, long skinny breads poking through the holes. On a bench in the middle of the street (there is no sign of a car or any form of transportation—what happens if someone wants to move a piano?), two old men smoke and sigh with every exhale. I peek in windows. *Salumeria* must be an Italian deli—there are little fish floating in oil, roasted red peppers, vats of green olives and wrinkly black ones, fat rounds of cheese, salamis hanging from the ceiling, strings of garlic and onions. Wouldn't James be frothing here? More stores. *Farmacia*. Drugstore. *Frutti-vendolo*. I love that musical word and try it out loud—*frutti-ven-dolo*. Women pick over peaches, plums, nectarines, tomatoes, exotic fruits I don't recognize—big meaty yellow things, small prickly green things—melons small as tennis balls and big as basketballs, bunches of gorgeous grapes. All this fruit is unceremoniously piled in wooden crates, perhaps straight from the farm.

Banco. Bank. I walk in. I know I can't shop without money, and I'm starving, dying to pop one of those juicy grapes into my mouth, panting over *il panetteria*, a bread store where the smells are heavenly. *"Buon giorno,"* I say to the only teller, an owl-faced man peering out from behind a small grated window. I put down ten dollars and read from my book, "Do you change . . . *puo cambiare* . . ." This trail-off technique works well. *"Sì,"* the man says, and counts out several bills in a rainbow of colors, money that looks like it's only good for Italian Monopoly. "Euros?" I ask. He frowns and scratches at his brush of a mustache. I wave the money, "Euros?" but as I do, I notice that "lire" is written on them. Lire. Twelve thousand, a fortune, and I gave him only ten dollars. How confusing. "Italy?" I say again, in case the country changed on me.

"Sì, Italia, signorina." He bursts out laughing.

"Grazie," I say.

"Molte grazie," he replies.

"Via Gravino. Dov'è Via Gravino?"

He sprays a torrent of Italian and flaps his hand in the direction I've been walking. I discern *"destro,"* I think I hear that word. I flip through the book. "Right." *Destro* means right. Via Gravino might be on the right. *"Grazie,"* I say again, giving the "r" a good spin. I'm beginning to enjoy saying thank you in Italian.

I stroll out and into *il panetteria*, drool over baskets of skinny crusty breads, round crackly wheat breads, little white rolls, olive rolls, some buns speckled with green, others with a confetti of red and green. Eventually I make a selection, pointing, hand over a bill, and get back bills and coins, who knows what. At the fruit stand I point at grapes and soon I have a bag of those, too. While I munch, a waiter beckons me to sit at an outdoor café. I shake my head. Another waiter scoots around him, carrying a small square tray containing six cups with foamy white tops. He delivers them to noisy tourists who push their maps aside to make room. Nearby, two slim men in black suits confer over tiny cups of coffee. I loiter nearby, wishing for English, but all the language escapes me and appears to be spoken at lightning speed. Moving along, I nearly fall into a trance over the spirited and relaxed way color is thrown about—houses painted burnt orange, tawny and coppery yellows, fuchsia, a clashing purple door, stripes and stenciled trims. Dad . . . I want to show Dad. He'd love this.

I guess my whole life I'll see things I want to show him. Although maybe this is a place he wants to show me. It is *his* puzzle.

Distracted by color, I collide with a small wooden kiosk. A man seated in a folding chair, his face obscured by the newspaper he's reading, lowers his paper, gives me the once-over, and raises it up again. *La Gazzetta dello Sport.* The front page, pink, is an eye-popping assault of type, which I scour, hoping to recognize a name, something, but no luck. The kiosk, papered with magazines for sale, makes a flashy and glossy collage. *Donna Moderna*, *Il Mondo*, *Tutto Motto* (judging from the photo, it's about motorcycles), *Cosmopolitan*. So there's an Italian edition. Next to the title, on the right, it says, "*Luglio 1990.*" *Luglio*, I saw that, somewhere I noticed . . . I swivel back to the man engrossed in the newspaper. Yes, next to the name, *La Gazzetta dello Sport*, in small type, there it is: 12 *Luglio* 1990. A date, it must be a date. I flip through my phrase book to "Months." *Luglio* is July. In Italian the day appears before the month, so according to that newspaper, today is July 12, 1990.

That's before I was born. That's the year before I was born.

I am wandering around in a year I've never lived in, in a village so ancient, Mel might be an expert on its sewage system.

The noisy gulls are back, announcing themselves with raucous barks. *Caw, caw, caw.* I look up, expecting a flock. Instead, a solitary seagull glides to a landing on a balcony railing. *Via Gravino.* A plaque with those words is affixed to the wall right next to the bird. Via Gravino. I held that sign in my palm—white lettering on yellow—and there it is. Only now do I realize that I'm at an intersection. Via Gravino begins here, *destro* (on the right), a street of tattered charm like the others, and I might have passed it right by, except for the bird.

I hurry down Via Gravino, searching faces, peering in windows, turning around again and again in case I've missed a clue, a sign. And then the street ends, curving into another. It just ends.

Panting with anxiety, I sink down on a bench, trying to quiet my heart. How could there be nothing? A tinkle of bells spooks me, but it's only a wind chime shivering in an open window. Two children squeal as they chase by, then I hear wings beating the air and jerk up to see the bird streak past a terraced stone path where my father is looking out at the view.

"Dad?" I leap up. "Dad!"

He swings around. His face lights up when he

spies me, and he raises his hand, our signal.

I can't see how to get to him. The stone terrace has great arches under it and it's high, as high as a third floor. "How?" I shout. "How?"

He points down. I tear into the passageway underneath the terrace, zigzagging between stone columns. There, in the shadow of an arch, nearly hidden from view, I spot the stairs. I race to them, skip up two and three at a time. I think I throw myself the final distance into his arms.

He squeezes me tight and lifts me off the ground. The thing about Dad, the thing I remember now, now that I'm feeling it, is that he's home.

I burrow into his shoulder. After all those hugs from virtual strangers like Harriet, hugs I've managed to steel myself through, I crash. "Take it easy," he whispers. Dad doesn't rush me, he never did, I remember that, too. He holds me while I soak his shirt with tears. He holds me until I wear out and wind down. Then he does this thing I'd forgotten. You know how your eyes get red and sore when you're crying your eyes out? Well, Dad kisses my eyes, first one, then the other, very gently—it's like the kiss of a butterfly—which is what he always did when I was inconsolable, like after he moved out. Finally he takes me by the shoulders and holds me at arm's distance. I remember and miss all at the same time his face appreciating mine. No one else loves so much to look at me.

"Hi there, my beauty."

"Daddy." And then it pours out, everything, finding him, running into the street, being so lonely, being the only one, needing to lie down all the time, everywhere, for no reason. He just listens while I blubber and carry on. I keep wiping my nose with my sleeve, and that makes me realize that we're both wearing blue work shirts because I'm wearing his clothes. "Nice outfit," says Dad, like he's reading my mind.

"I have all your clothes. Mom tried to make me throw things out, but I wouldn't."

We walk over to a bench, which I didn't realize

was a bench because it blends completely into the terrace. Three misshapen rocks, one long and lumpy balancing on the other two—a bench of stones that could be as old as the Temple of Dendur, the perfect place for us. As we rest there, I happen to look down and notice my shoes next to Dad's. Our feet side by side. There's something so sad about that.

Dad takes my hand, and that makes me even sadder. "Your hand's cold," he tells me. He always says that. He's said it to me a million times. Dad has this completely fierce, crushing grip. I don't shake hands with him, I never did, obviously, because he's my dad, but now I'm recalling that Jenna told me that BlueBerry said her hand nearly disintegrated the first time she shook hands with him.

"Remember how you were the champion arm-wrestler in college?" I haven't thought about that in ages either, or that when I was little we always arm-wrestled. "You let me beat you."

"No, you won."

"You always said that, and I thought I was so strong. Dad, tell me what happened? Did it hurt? Were you scared?"

"When?"

"You know."

He shakes his head.

"Come on, this can't be like *Little Women*, where I hunt and hunt but the details are never revealed."

"You'll find nothing here you don't already know."

"What?"

He gives me the MLS. No kidding. Me, the big MLSer, gets one back, and believe me, he's better at it than me. I search his eyes for a clue—the eyes are the key to everything—but his remain opaque, and his mysterious half smile gives away nothing.

"I don't get it."

"You will." He tucks my hair behind my ear, where it won't stay, and straightens my shirt—his shirt—on my shoulders. I am totally rumpled. I wish I could bottle this feeling of having Dad tidy me up. And let me tell you, my dad is handsome. He has the warmest, most soulful brown eyes, and his face is so open to feeling. When he smiles, he could melt ice. When he's serious, his intensity positively radiates. A photograph can convey the specifics; it helps with the history—that Dad's nose is crooked, for instance. He broke it in a fistfight when he was ten. My dad, the tough kid. But a photo never captures charisma. Definition (mine): having charm enough to fuel a rocket. Right now he's telling me something, and my mind is wandering into how happy I am, how lucky, how amazing. I have to ask him to repeat. "What, Dad?"

"You don't get to know what death is or isn't. No one gets that."

"But I'm here. No one gets *that* but me."

He laughs. Hearing him laugh is fantastic. Laughs are original, each person's, don't you think that's true, and they are extremely hard to recall. Almost impossible. His rumbles, like it's coming out of a bass drum. I'm loving that so much that I almost miss the bad news. "The ordinary mysteries of life—those you're stuck with," he says.

Death is a mystery for sure. Death is one colossal mystery. "But I'm scared. If I'm scared, how can I live?"

"Exactly."

"Exactly? That's not an answer, Dad." He's turned into Confucius, dispensing little sayings with no explanations. He used be the great expounder. "I'll find nothing?"

"Nothing that you don't already know."

"Why am I here, to build up my muscles?"

"Is that a bad idea?"

"Be serious."

"I am. Come on, banana, look at the view."

Dad leans forward and rests his arms on the terrace wall. I do the same, and together like big birds, we survey the area. We're at the far edge of the cove, high above, and from this perch we can appreciate the whole landscape of Dad's puzzle.

Below, the houses huddled around the cove, the beached dinghies, the cluster of seaside tables shaded by umbrellas in jaunty colors. It's thrilling to see the whole panorama for the first time. My hard work brought it to life. Most amazing is the confirmation once and for all that we're in the puzzle, because there are no blues. Wherever land meets sky, there's a jigsaw horizon of giant knobs and indentations as if our whole world, Dad and my private world, has a fanciful turreted wall around it. The GWW seeps through the ins-and-outs and appears to coat the entire sky with a gray, filmy glaze. Out in the sea, well, there is no sea except for the little boat bobbing in its blue lagoon with lacy puzzle edges. Instead of water there's a steamy mist so light, it might be rising off a cup of hot tea.

"Remember, you waved to me when I was in that boat."

"I did?"

"You must remember—you were at the hotel." I

point to the building, but he's not interested. Did death give Dad amnesia?

"Puzzle light is unlike any other," he says, "because it's fixed."

"Except for the GWW." I explain that I call that spooky stuff the Great Woolly White. "The more of the puzzle I completed, the thinner it got, I guess because it occupied less space."

"You did the puzzle?" He sounds surprised.

"Who else? Now the GWW is wispy and romantic, tantalizing, don't you think?"

Dad nods. He gets the mood.

"At first I thought the puzzle was Ireland, but then I fell into that café, the one with the grape vines on the wall. By the way, remember that place-mat in your office, the watercolor of grapes? Mom stole it."

"Really?"

"It was on your wall and then it was on Mel's."

"So that means she stole it?"

"What else?"

"You tell me."

"What do you mean?"

Dad just smoothes my hair.

"I can't believe I have to grow up with Mel. He's the un-Dad. Mom married him as a reaction."

"They always seemed happy when I bumped into them in town."

"They were probably . . ."

"What?" says Dad.

"Nothing." I was going to say pretending, but I'm thinking about that stupid game they play where they get excited about commercials and laugh their heads off. Also the nickname Booper. Dumb, but you'd never call a guy Booper unless you were sweet on him. "You never said that before."

"What?"

"Anything nice about Mom and Mel. Anything really. You acted as if Mel didn't exist."

"I have a different perspective now," he says.

I guess that's a death joke. "Dad, they're not artists like us."

"No?"

"No! God, Dad, you're not agreeing with any-thing I say."

"I'm not disagreeing."

"You're doing something."

"Calm down," he says. "Are you hungry? Why don't we get a gelato?"

Showing off my new muscles, I descend the deep terrace steps without a wince. We stroll through the town, cozy together. "I wish she didn't send me to that idiotic school."

"It's a good school."

He sure has changed his opinions, or did he always think that? Is that something I already know? Since I'm supposed to know everything? "Who pays for it?" he remarks. That is absolutely not a question, because we both know the answer.

"You couldn't, Dad, you're an artist." I point out the obvious.

We lapse into silence. If you want to think, walk. Mom always says that, and I never paid attention, but it's true. My mind drifts. Information rearranges itself. Maybe it's the squeak of our shoes on the cobblestones, or the comfort of my arm linked through Dad's, or everyone around me speaking a language I don't understand so why try, or simply the happiness of being with Dad, but suddenly I know. "The watercolor was Mom's. You stole it from her."

He laughs. "Now *I* stole it?"

"Okay, not stole, but you kept it when you got divorced. I bet you didn't tell her. Because when she saw it, she was surprised." I'd been preoccupied with concealing Dad's gift. I assumed she'd never been in Dad's studio before. She probably hadn't, but she did take a serious pause and dart straight to the grapes. "Mom painted that, didn't she?"

Dad grins. He's proud of me, as if I've shown him a report card with straight As.

So Dad liked that watercolor not because it was a painting on a placemat. He just liked it. Or maybe he especially liked it because Mom did it. Every time he took a break from work and looked up, that's what he saw.

I have to think about that.

"Why doesn't Mom paint anymore?" I throw that out, but I know he won't tell me. I'm wondering if I already know that, too. I mean, if you consider what you know, you also have to consider if there's something you've refused to know. Why did she stop painting?

A hairpin turns wends us into a street so narrow that, to appreciate the striped and patterned houses and the crooked tile roofs, we have to crane our heads way back. We're in a skinny museum with huge colorful canvases on both sides, but no way to achieve distance to get a decent view.

Ahead, where the houses end, a ribbon of GWW curls in and snakes toward us. I grab Dad's hand now, because it looks as if we're bound for oblivion, but we walk right through, and as soon as we spill out of needle street, we're on the wharf, big and open and inviting except for a steam-pit cove. The smell is distinctive, low tide. Low tide and no water. How strange. A boy races by. I watch him until he catches up with a cluster of tourists around the stone church. Hey, I built that church, piece by piece.

The hotel turns out to have a name, Il Fiore di Mare, scripted in white neon above the door. I drag Dad down the quay, but when I reach the hotel, I want simply to lay my hand against the wall. The stucco feels cool and rough. I don't know why I need to do this. The plaster has faded unevenly, its lovely plum color mottled and spotted, cracks everywhere. When I lift my hand, pink dust sparkles on my palm.

I glance up at the second-story window. The window is open now, shutters thrown back. "From there," I show him. "You waved at me from there."

"Where do you want to sit?" asks Dad.

I search for another touchstone, the tangerine-colored umbrella. On a second go-round I spot it, folded closed, cinched with a thick cord. I point to the table nearest it and push Dad to hurry over. I'm wondering about the smudges in the puzzle, items merely hinted at, too small or nearly hidden. On the round white table—the one that umbrella must have shaded—sits a single white ceramic mug, a trace of foam on the inside, coffee half drunk, lipstick smeared on the rim. A red flannel jacket flops over the chair back. I'm about to snatch it for a closer look when a waiter pinches it by the collar, tosses it over his arm, collects the mug, and wipes the table clean.

"Due gelati, per favore," says my dad as we sit. *"Cioccolati."*

I chatter about Jenna and James, making Dad laugh, which I love to do, describing Signor Chef flipping his oven mitts, the crazy chicken valentine. I tell him about Harriet the Honker trashing the poison collage, Rocco and Leo the Lizard. "That camp is prison," I insist. I omit Simon, but the whole time I'm bringing Dad up-to-date on everything, everything that's happened since he died, I consider how to slide Simon in without setting off curiosity alarms. I never figure out how, so I don't tell Dad everything. I guess this is the official beginning of his not knowing stuff.

The gelato is delicious. I stir it into soup and eat it by dipping the spoon, holding up the spoon so the soup drips back into the bowl, and licking the residue off the spoon back. This is positively the slowest way to consume ice cream. I always did it when I was little and it was time for Dad to take me back to Mom's and I didn't want to leave him.

"Will I ever stop being sad?"

"The blues are the hardest."

"Dad, don't joke."

"I'm not, honey. It's the truth."

"I don't get why you would give me this weird town in Italy. I was sure it was Ireland. Wasn't it amazing that I discovered the puzzle?"

"You can't control things after you die."

That bugs me and I can't explain why. I throw myself back in my chair and glare.

"Do you want to get mad at me?" he asks.

"I don't know."

"Will it make it easier?"

I know what he's referring to. Leaving. "Did you have a premonition? Is that why you finished them early?"

"Finished what early?"

He's being so dense. "My beautiful carved box. The puzzle. You finished them before my birthday. You never finished things ahead of time."

I think he's pondering that observation, running it through his brain maze, but then I realize, no. He seems to wilt. He's here with me but almost not. He's moving away without moving a muscle. "Dad?"

He reaches out to touch my face. "You'll figure out the rest."

"Can't I come back?"

"No," he tells me in a whisper so faint it could be the wind. "Go."

I don't think my legs will walk, but I hear the chair scrape the ground as I stand. The gull is calling—

that noisy raucous bird demands my attention. I watch it swoop by and vanish into the plumy mist rising from an empty sea.

When I turn back for one last look, I'm smack in front of Mom's front door, and the only thing in front of my face is a big brass door knocker. A medieval lion. Mel installed it when he moved in. I don't know what to do, so I lift the heavy ring and rap.

"Who's there?" Mom calls.

"Me."

She opens the door. She's wearing a striped apron and wielding a wooden spoon. "What's wrong?" she says instantly. She opens her arms and I fall into them. "What? What is it, sweetie?"

I whimper into her shoulder.

She holds me tight. "You miss your dad?"

I whimper more and she clasps me tighter.

"You're stabbing me, what's this?" Mom separates to see what's jabbing her ribs—my mini Italian phrase book. "Are you studying Italian?"

I sniffle. "No, Jenna's boyfriend is."

"Your dad and I were in Italy before you were born. In this tiny coastal town so innocent—" She stops. Her body tenses, her face stiffens. Boy, do I recognize that jarring halt, the instinct to resist a feeling so powerful it could mow you down. She takes her time, letting emotions recede before confiding. "It was the most romantic time of my life."

She pulls me into the house and swings her arm around my shoulder, keeping me close as we walk to the kitchen. "Come on, come with me. Are you hungry? What can I get you?"

"I don't know." I can't keep the wail out of my voice.

"Sit down right here." She pulls out a chair and I sink into it. My head feels wobbly. I have to lay it on the table.

Mom pulls a chair around right next to mine. Over and over she strokes my hair. She has a feather touch. My eyelids droop and finally close. My brain gives up and shuts down. I wish I could rest here forever.

Eventually she gets up and I hear rustling, so I look. She's tasting something in a big pot. She sprinkles in spices, salt and pepper, tastes it again, and lowers the heat. "Chili," she says. "It will be done soon." She hangs up her apron.

"Do you want to watch the light, Mom?"

"The light?"

"The sunset."

"What a wonderful idea."

We go upstairs. Off her bedroom the deck has a brand-new wicker couch. With my legs tucked up and my head resting on Mom's shoulder, we snuggle while the sun melts on the horizon. It looks like an egg, sunny side up.

30

I can't do the blues. Every time I try, I break down. Sobbing, wailing, moaning. Sounds come out of me I've never heard before. I roll around on my bed, muffle the noise with my pillow, mop my face with a towel, and try again. More sobs. I didn't know eyes could produce so many tears. Scientifically speaking. My chest hurts and my nose is sore from blowing it. I don't want to finish the puzzle. I know I can't go back, but I don't want to go forward either. The blues are good-bye, the final closing of the gate, good-bye to Dad.

After crying enough tears to bust a dam, I concentrate for a moment here, a moment there, and then I get caught up because the blues are so challenging.

To make matches, I have to be sensitive to nuance because there are no obvious clues. With the pastels, for instance, all those baby blues, it isn't just that I have to hunt for tinges of pink or the barest hint of lilac or the tiniest brush of white that might be a cloud. I have to see the emotion in color—the sunniness, the flatness, the joy, the calm, the ache, the sigh. Sometimes I can't rely on color, only shape—slight angles, fractional differences in depth or curves. The blues sharpen me. They make me see things I never saw before. They force me to see in new ways.

Mom and Dad were in Vernazza together in July, aka *Luglio*, 1990. July. Nine months before I was born. Once I ponder those facts, I understand Dad: His obtuseness when I said he'd waved to me from the hotel window; his surprise that *I* did the puzzle; his confusion when I raved about how amazing it was that he'd finished it early. Dad never finished anything early. Like everything else he did, this was late. By the time he completed it, their marriage was over. I guess he wrapped it up and put it away. It had been stashed under that desk for years. The wrapping paper wasn't recycled. It was old.

The puzzle and box were for Mom. An act of love, as Jenna said. He carved my name, Frances Anne, because I happened there. Me. Their creation.

They had me because they were happy together. It's comforting to know that. It's comforting to know that my parents loved each other, even if it wasn't forever.

Dad made these gifts for Mom and that's who's going to get them, but how? I can't leave the puzzle on the floor. What is Mom going to do with a completed jigsaw puzzle as large as the kitchen table? That will be her problem, not mine, although I searched the web and it turns out you can have puzzles framed. As for that gorgeous box, she can use it for jewelry or for pictures of me—I could suggest that. I think she'll like having the mementoes of Dad.

Dad wasn't right about something. All that "trust the eyes" stuff. My eyes led me to misunderstanding and wrong conclusions because here's something else I figure out while I'm doing the blues: The eyes see only what the heart lets them. Take Mom's listening to Dad's hideous pennywhistle music on that afternoon when we cleared out his house. She was relishing those bird twitters, she was a million miles away, maybe thinking of some dreamy time when he played her that music, maybe when they were lolling about on a Sunday afternoon or had just brought me home from the hospital and they thought they'd delight my baby ears. But what did I see when she tapped her foot in time? Irritation. A frenemy in motion.

If you have to ask the big question—what rules,

brain or heart?—you have to say heart. Which is why life is an illusion. I mean, there are some facts. My dad died. But the sense I make of what happens after or what came before—that's my heart, filtering, judging. My heart was always biased toward Dad.

I want to ask Mom about Dad, so I wait for a cozy moment. We're sorting his things in the garage, up to our elbows in dump treasures. I'm trying to make a more serious attempt at parting with his belongings. "You stopped painting because of me, didn't you, Mom? Someone had to earn the money."

"I love my life, Frannie."

"But that wasn't fair of him." This is really troubling me. "Was Dad selfish?"

Mom is combing through ceramic bits and pieces, someone's broken patio tiles. She takes her time, stacking the tiles in a paper bag, folding over and creasing the top. "Sometimes I thought so. Sometimes I was furious at him. No . . ." She thinks some more. "The truth is, I was so resentful that until he died, I forgot why I fell in love with him to begin with. All that passion."

"If he was so passionate, why did you get divorced?"

"I changed when we had you. I thought he would too."

"How changed?"

"Frannie, looking at it now with different eyes—"

"You mean, with your heart. Looking with your heart."

"Yes. Your dad wasn't selfish. It was just that, for him, art was as essential as breathing."

I wonder if I'm like that.

Mom decides we need some refreshment, so she heads into the house. I chase after. "Why did you give the painting to Mel? A memento of your romantic time with Dad? How could you?"

She stops, a bit stunned. "That painting came out of an experience, but once I completed it, it became its own thing. A work of art. You're an artist, you understand."

"I guess."

"I love the painting and I love Mel. I can't explain it any more clearly than that."

Maybe Mom will give the puzzle to Mel too. Until that second, it never occurred to me that this puzzle could end up in the hands of Booper.

I have no control over that, do I? Dad said that after you die you have no control, but it seems to me that you don't have much control when you're alive, either. I mean, look who Jenna fell for. And whoever thought I'd feel at peace gazing into the eyes of a guy who eats art. That was so peculiar, I'd rather not think about it. And Mom. She didn't have any control about falling in or out of love with Dad.

I make a drawing. A patio table shaded by an umbrella, a half-drunk cappuccino, a jacket thrown over a chair. Perhaps on vacation in an Italian village called Vernazza, a man goes off by himself exploring. From high up on a stone terrace he takes a photo of the whole vista—the cove, the village, the hotel, rooftops receding up the mountain, and a seaside café. The café is barely visible from afar—a jumble of patio umbrellas, that's all—but he particularly notices a bright tangerine umbrella tilted at a sharp angle. He returns, and from his hotel window, in this much closer view, he sees the things he missed. Details, people. Under that tangerine umbrella, shaded from the sun, sits the woman he loves. "Laura," he calls. He raises his hand, their signal. In her haste, running to meet him, she forgets her jacket, leaves her coffee half drunk.

I'm not sure what I'll call it. Maybe B.F. Before Frannie.

31

Testing its stability, Harriet gives the ladder a shake. "Go ahead," she tells Simon, who presses his foot on the first rung and gradually transfers his entire weight. The rung bends but holds, and Simon, a hammer tucked into his belt, ascends to the barn loft. As he treads across, the loft floor groans. Bits of hay between the slats dislodge and sprinkle us. I keep expecting his foot to slip between the slats and snare him like a bear in a trap. Simon pries off the board that seals the window, rips off the plastic, bright light floods in, and we're ready to launch.

On this last day of camp, Harriet has decided that the Egg Drop is the big event. The campers have invited their parents, whose cars jam the parking lot and stretch along the side of the road. I invited Jenna because she's been sad about James, but when I leave the barn, Jenna is bounding toward me with a gleeful grin (translation: He's back). Which is self-evident. James ambles alongside her, carrying four dozen eggs.

"The eggs are here," shouts Rocco.

"Thanks for bringing them," I tell Jenna and James.

There's a pause long enough for my hair to grow an inch. Finally Jenna chirps, "Hi, I'm Jenna," and Rocco volunteers, "He's Simon, this is Leo," and I realize that Simon is hanging out behind me. "Hey," says Simon.

"I got great eggs." James flips a box open.

"Are those dinosaur eggs?" asks Rocco.

They are very large and they are green. "Jumbo organic," says James. "From free-range chickens."

"Why are they green?" asks Hazel.

"The chickens ate only alfalfa grass," James says. "They make a fantastic omelet."

"We're going to launch them, didn't you tell him we're going to launch them?" I ask Jenna.

"Oops," says Jenna.

"Launch?" James appears mystified.

"They're going in parachutes," says Simon.

"Everyone's parachute should be in the barn," I shout. "We're starting in fifteen minutes."

"Parachutes?" says James. "No way."

Fortunately Harriet sails up at that moment. She thanks James, whom she knows from Cobweb, whips the egg boxes out of his hands, deposits them in mine, and shoos me and Simon back to the barn.

"How do you want to do this?" Simon asks me.

"I don't know."

This riveting communication is our first exchange since we felt each other's faces. I've been avoiding him. As we walk across the field, I know he's matching me stride for stride. It's impossible not to be aware of his hulking body next to me even if I'm not looking. Besides, his meaty arm swings to and fro, invading my peripheral vision.

Since I contribute nothing, he suggests that I go up the ladder and he'll hand me the parachutes.

I should go up the ladder. I should stand in the open loft window. I should send the parachutes and their egg passengers to their destinies. "No problem," I hear myself reply.

As we're about to enter the barn, Simon says, "Wait one second," and sprints over to the tennis court, where the ENP has set up a refreshment table with juice and a bunch of desserts contributed by the moms. The whole activity must have exhausted her, because she's sitting in a folding chair while Pearl waves a fan to cool her. Simon downs several glasses of juice and chats. They must be making a date, because when she talks to him, she bothers to stand.

No way am I watching this close encounter, so I

head into the barn. The floor is strewn with the campers' creations, all the crazy concoctions of tissue paper, glue, and toothpicks. I have to negotiate my way carefully.

I test the ladder, giving it a shake the way Harriet did, and start up. On about the fifth rung I start down, almost miss the last rung in my haste, shove parachutes away to clear space. Not until I am flat on the floor, on my back, in a major timeout, does the panic ebb. I hear Lark declare, "She's horizontal."

"What?" That's Simon's voice.

"That's what she calls lying down. Hey, why do I have to leave?"

I hear the barn door slide close and see Simon looming over me. "What's wrong?"

"How can you live if you're scared?"

"Heavy," says Simon. He squats down next to me. "Is that one of those questions with no answer?"

"Maybe."

He wrinkles his nose. He looks as if he's sniffing,

but my guess is he's thinking. "What are you scared of?" he says.

"Death. What else?"

"Are you sure it's not—"

"What?"

"Life. You've got to live, no choice, so the question is how? If you're not scared, it's got to be more fun."

"Fun?" I hadn't thought about fun.

"Anyway, worrying is a waste because there's no predicting."

"What?"

"Anything."

Outside, Lark provides a news report: "She's resting." Harriet tells her to hush and continues blasting through the bullhorn about how the campers made the parachutes, and how proud of them she is, and that I am a brilliant arts and crafts counselor. How can a person be brilliant at arts and crafts? It's hardly an IQ thing. Meanwhile Simon's face is coming closer. Is he checking to see if my pupils are dilated or if I need the paramedics?

He kisses me.

You know how in the movies when a man and a woman kiss, it looks as if they're swallowing each other's mouths? As if they're motivated by hunger. Well, this is nothing like that. This is the opposite. His lips graze mine, then they're gone. It's as if he was scouting the territory, checking the lay of the land. I'm about to open my eyes, thinking the whole event is over, when his lips are back, lingering longer, off and back again, this time with a few tender nibbles thrown in. What is this? This is so original. I'm quivering. Did he invent it?

I open my eyes. Simon is sitting back on his heels, breathing heavily.

"*Grazie*," I say.

Grazie? How deranged is that? Why do I thank him for kissing me, much less thank him in Italian? How utterly mortifying. But Simon only responds by putting out his hand. I take it, and he hauls me up. As soon as I'm standing, he's going to grab me, or maybe I'm going to grab him, I might be mixed up about that.

"What's going on?" Harriet booms from outside, which halts the fun.

Simon climbs the ladder. Without discussing it, we agree that this is the better deployment of our workforce. There's some clapping. I suppose he's appeared in the loft window.

After I hand up a box of eggs and Lark's lion, I slide open the barn door so I can view the launch-ings.

Out glides her lion, its mane fluttering. In a swarm the entire camp and their parents follow the trajectory. It hesitates in the air above the tennis court, swaying back and forth, before making a slow descent onto a plate of cupcakes. Harriet checks the mouth of the lion, where Lark has stashed the egg. Thumbs up. The egg survived.

Lark dances around, waving her lion. "I'm going to win," she crows, which causes Harriet to raise her bullhorn and announce that there are no winners.

"This isn't a win thing," she claims.

One after another, Simon sets the parachutes loose. The Barbies' honeymoon cruise, as they call their blue-and-silver-starred boat, does a dance, spinning in place, and then collapses. The egg breaks. The Barbies turn wild and stomp the boat to pieces. Gregor's bomb pleases him no end when it torpedoes south and slams into a rock. Seymour's parachute is a mountain, at least that's what I always thought—an all-beige mound of tissue— but this week he covered the peak with a bit of dark-brown tissue. As soon as it commences its disastrous journey straight down, Hazel yelps, "It's a breast," and slaps her hand over her mouth as if she's said something shocking. All the boys shriek with laughter and sock one another. Seymour thrusts his fist into the air. The parachute crashes and the egg shatters. Pearl's butterfly swiftly blows out of camp. On its gradual descent into the middle of the road, a pickup truck slows down, and a hand reaches out the window, catches the butterfly, and takes off with it. The egg tumbles out, however, and cracks. Hazel's daisy has the most graceful flight. All the petals flutter as it lightly bounces along a gentle wind, then alights on some tall grass and rests atop it. The egg survives.

Rocco scrambles by me into the barn and is up the ladder before I can catch him. "Hey, you forgot the egg," I hear Simon say, as Rocco yells, "Go Leo."

As his centipede parachute wafts out, the many legs loosely dangling, I see a tiny triangular head bobbing above the tissue-paper basket that Rocco has built on the centipede's back. The parachute catches a swift gust and picks up speed.

"Leo's flying," shouts Rocco.

"Leo's on the bug," the Barbies broadcast.

In two jumps Simon is down the ladder, and we streak across the field, leading the pack. The centipede dips and rises. Has Leo tumbled out already? No one can tell, but we all pound the ground in pursuit. The bug stops midair, hovers while we watch breathlessly, and plummets. We rush to the crash site. Leo's guts will be spilled, his body in smithereens. I clutch Simon's arm as we close in on the pile of crumpled tissue. Remarkably, the basket is intact and Leo remains in it. But he's still. Utterly still.

Everyone erupts, screaming at Rocco. "Killer!" "Murderer!"

"I'm not. He loved it. He flew. He's the first flying lizard."

"He's dead, dummy," says Lark.

"No hitting." That's a grownup voice. I don't look, but it's probably Rocco and Lark's dad, scolding Lark. There is lots of sniffling.

I open my hand next to Leo. Slowly he creeps onto it. His lids rise, descend, and rise again.

"Leo lives!" I shout. "He lives."

Everyone cheers so loudly, the trees shake.

Simon places Leo on his shoulder and Leo rides like a champion to the refreshment table. Harriet beams. "Great job with the parachutes, Frannie."

All the kids drag their parents over to meet me. My hand is nearly shaken off. Jenna sits in James's lap and feeds him a cupcake. A cloud moves across the sky, and the sun flickers in and out, casting bright beams and shadows, turning Harriet's hair from flaming red to brown and back again.

Simon, eating Oreos, has ten campers hanging off him. He's a human jungle gym. "Hey," he says, "who wants to canoe?"

The campers jump up and down, me, me, me, me.

"Me." I raise my hand.

We all troop down to the lake.

He's not my type. I could never be with a guy who isn't an artist.

But maybe Simon is an artist. An artist when it comes to kissing. A kissing artist.

I have to think about that.

Author's Note

Vernazza is an ancient village at the base of rocky cliffs in an area of northern Italy known as Cinque Terre (Five Lands). Generally speaking the town exists as I have described it with steep and narrow streets, a small muddy cove, seaside cafés, and a large stone church. However, specific details—the name of a street or hotel, a particular shop, the color of a shutter—are romantic rather than accurate, memories of a visit I took one fall with cherished friends and the man I love.

Acknowledgments

Writing a book is a journey, and I always need help so I don't get lost. Barbara Sjogren, the wonderful art teacher at the Calhoun School in New York City, was so helpful that I was actually able to construct a parachute for the egg drop as well as write about it. Julia and Richard Gregson talked me into a hiking trip to Italy, and even though I could stand the hiking for only one day, I couldn't have written this book without the experience. My husband, Jerome Kass, the world's best storyteller, shared as he always does his awesome skills and unerring emotional compass. Naomi Touger took terrific photographs. Lorraine Bodger always gives me excellent editorial advice. My agent, Lynn Nesbit, is perfect. As for my editor, Laura Geringer . . . occasionally in my writer's life, I have been blessed with great good fortune. She is extraordinary and I thank her from the bottom of my heart.